CHASING

THE

KING

BY
JOSHUA STEIN
www.scobre.com

Scobre Press Corporation
2255 Calle Clara
La Jolla, CA 92037

Scobre Press books may be purchased for educa-
tional, business or sales promotional use.

First Scobre edition published 2003.

Edited by Ramey Temple
Cover Art by Larry Salk
Cover Layout by Michael Lynch

ISBN 0-9741695-7-9

www.scobre.com

To all the dreamers...

We at Scobre Press are proud to bring you another book in our "Dream Series." In case this is your first Scobre book, here's what we're all about. The goal of Scobre is to influence young people by entertaining them with books about athletes who act as role models. The moral dilemmas facing the athletes in a Scobre story run parallel to situations facing many young people today. After reading a Scobre book, our hope is that young people will be able to respond to adversity in their lives in the same heroic fashion as the athletes depicted in our books.

This book is about Jason Skidder, a kid from San Francisco who thought he had everything in his life figured out. He was destined to grow up and go to high school with all of his friends. He also carried the hope that he would eventually have the chance to play soccer professionally. But as you will soon find out in "Chasing the King," things don't always go as they are planned.

This book offers an in-depth look at the game of soccer and what the sport means to two drastically different cultures. "Chasing the King" is also about how one young man reacts to change in his life.

We invite you now to come along with us, sit down, get comfortable, and read a book that will dare you to dream. Scobre dedicates this book to all the people who are chasing down their own dreams. We're sure that Skids will inspire you to reach for the stars.

Here's Skids and "Chasing the King."

To my supportive family and close friends. And to Slim, who, in ten years, gave me a lifetime of friendship and so much more.

CHAPTER ONE

SWERVE BALL

I froze at the bottom of the stairs.

"What was that?" I asked.

"Can you come upstairs for a minute? Mom and I need to talk to you." Dad repeated.

I gulped loudly. I knew something important was about to happen. The last time Dad spoke those words, he told me that Mom was pregnant. My sister Keri turned out to be pretty cool. So I knew the news wasn't guaranteed to be bad, just important. I climbed the stairs and tried to guess what was in store for me.

I turned the corner into my parents' room. I noticed a happy look in both of their eyes. I took a seat in Mom's favorite chair and began rocking. I started to get a little excited. "So what's the news, another kid on the way?"

"No." Mom giggled.

I stared blankly at her. "What then?"

"I'm just going to say this, Jason." Dad continued. "I've been offered a job in Rio de Janeiro, Brazil."

I stopped rocking in Mom's chair. "What?" I whispered. I was confused as I leaned in closer to Dad. "What do you mean?"

Dad's voice grew deeper. "Well, I've accepted this job, Jason—in Brazil. I start next month. I'm going to move down there and start looking for a house right away." He paused. "Then you, Keri, and Mom will join me."

"In Brazil?" I was totally confused, even shocked. I could feel Mom and Dad staring at me. They were waiting for a response. I was frozen. I couldn't speak. *Where the heck was Brazil, anyway? Do the people there speak English? What about my soccer teams?* "What about…" I started with this last thought. I couldn't finish my sentence without crying. So I stopped.

Mom broke the silence. "We know that this will be a tough move for you. Especially with your friends and…"

I never heard Mom finish. I started to feel dizzy and ran down the stairs and out of the house. I only stopped to grab my soccer ball. What started as a normal Sunday had turned into the worst day of my life. How could I leave San Francisco? This was my home. I felt betrayed. I was mad at my parents for not giving me any warning. I was nervous about a future in a strange country.

I walked through the hilly streets of our neighborhood and thought about Brazil. I'd heard of it before. But I wanted a picture, some idea of what my life would be like. Brazil. Let's see—Pelé, the Amazon River, and South America. I tossed these three around in my head. The only one I cared much about was Pelé, the greatest soccer player of all time. He'd led Brazil to three World Cup championships. At seventeen, he became the youngest player to score a goal in the World Cup. Brazil had Pelé going for it, but not much else.

Mom and Dad had seen Pelé play once. Suddenly, I remembered that my parents had met one another in Brazil. They'd spent two years there before I was born. So that's why we're moving to Brazil!

I rounded the corner onto Nineteenth Street and stepped into Dolores Park. I couldn't imagine anything more magical than my home. It was a crisp afternoon. The sun was moving toward the ocean and the park lights flickered on. I looked down at my most loyal friend—an old soccer ball. I kicked the ball a few feet in front of me. I had my first positive thought about Brazil. *At least they take their soccer seriously down there.* I lifted the ball onto the tip of my right foot. Then I dropped it softly onto my knee where I began juggling. I alternated between my left and right. My mind wandered: 1, 2, 3...*Brazil, China, Russia, it was all the same to me.* 12, 13, 14...*How could*

Dad make me leave my friends? 23, 24, 25…*And my soccer teams too!* 26, 27, 28…*Would they even miss me?* This question broke my focus. The ball skipped off the outside of my left foot.

"Twenty nine, not bad Skids," a voice called out from behind me. Nobody ever called me by my given name, Jason Tyler Skidder. It had been simply "Jay" up until the fourth grade. Since then, everyone had been calling me Skids.

I spun around and saw Kevin Hoover.

"What's up Bones?" I asked, calling Kevin by his nickname.

"Not much," he replied. "Huge win yesterday."

I nodded and forced a smile. I kicked the ball crisply to his right foot. A moment later we fell into touch passing. It was impossible for two soccer players to look at a ball without kicking it.

The events of the last hour had shaken me up. I'd almost forgotten about yesterday's big game. In addition to playing on our high school teams, Kevin and I were members of the under-sixteen Bayside United team. Bayside United brought together the best talent in Northern California. Kevin, our goalie, was tall with great quickness. I was small, with decent speed, and usually played midfield.

Yesterday's championship game had been a tough contest against a team from Arizona. They never quit. We eventually won, but not before Arizona scored eight minutes into the game.

I remembered that goal as if it just happened. One of their midfielders made a strong run up the left sideline. He sent a high cross into the middle of the goal box. Once I saw him take off, I raced after him. I stopped myself around the eighteen-foot line. The ball made its way toward the goal. I tried to get my head on it, but I couldn't reach. The leather barely touched my hair, but didn't change direction. Luckily, Kevin was behind me. I was sure he'd make the play—he always did. But just as he jumped up to grab the ball, someone banged into him. Kevin's lower body crumpled. The ball passed just over his arms. It landed on the forehead of an Arizona player, who calmly headed it into the empty net.

We were able to tie it up before halftime on a goal that I assisted. We then got the go-ahead goal from my friend, Kyle. He was the best player on our team. With four minutes left, he proved it. He ran through four Arizona defenders easily and blasted a shot that looked like a bullet, not a soccer ball. Their goalie had no chance.

Winning that tournament was big. It ensured our team a place in the Championships in Florida in four months. I'd been looking forward to that trip for over a year. But with this crazy Brazil news, everything had changed. I didn't know if I would be in America in four months—forget Florida. I came back to reality and passed the ball back to Kevin. "You played a great game yesterday, Bones." I smiled, "Even if you did have that clumsy fall."

"You think that weak foot of yours can back up your big mouth, Skids?" Bones shot back smiling. "Penalty kicks—best out of five for a soda?"

"You're on," I said, grabbing the ball.

Bones and I had been through this routine a thousand times. He grabbed a metal trash can and placed it about fifteen feet from an old tree. I ran back about twenty feet and positioned the ball.

As good as Bones was in goal, penalty kicks were pretty easy. A pro soccer player makes about seventy-five percent of penalty kicks. I was no professional, but I liked my odds of making three of five to beat Bones. I jogged slowly toward the first ball and could taste the soda in my mouth.

Head down. Left foot—plant. Swing your body through the ball. I'd done it a million times before. My first kick came screaming off my right foot at exactly the angle I'd planned. To my surprise, Bones dove left right away. His fingertips barely touched the ball, knocking it into the metal trash can. The can went flying and the ball came to a stop.

One nothing, Bones.

Luck, I thought. I ran over to get the ball while Bones repositioned the dented trash can. Again, I jogged slowly to the ball and nailed a shot toward the tree, our right goalpost. *This one will get through,* I thought. But there was Bones again. Like a cat, he jumped left. This time, he caught the ball.

Two nothing, Bones.

Without saying a word, he rolled the ball back to me.

"Are you kidding me with that save?" I wondered aloud. I reset the ball. I looked at Bones straight in his eyes. I ran at the ball and hit it squarely with my right foot. This one didn't have the proper angle and Bones easily knocked it away. He then flicked the ball to me and winked. "One orange soda please."

I walked over to the vending machine and returned with two cold sodas.

"You were giving it away with your eyes." Bones greeted me as I took a seat next to him on a bench.

"I've got a lot on my mind right now." I began thinking about Brazil.

"Excuses, excuses." Bones said, waiting for me to smile. I stared straight ahead. He knew something was up. "What's wrong?"

I decided that Bones would be the first friend to hear the bad news. "Well, I don't know all the details yet." I didn't know what to say. "I—I'm moving to Brazil."

Kevin's jaw dropped, "Where?"

"Brazil," I continued. "I don't get it either. My Mom and Dad just told me. I'm still trying to figure everything out."

Kevin looked uncomfortable. He tried to be upbeat, "I read about Rio in my brother's surf magazine. They've got great beaches."

His comment annoyed me. "I don't care. Are you even listening? I'm leaving. All my friends, Hilltop High School, our Bayside United team, this neighborhood. Who cares about the stupid beaches?" The more I talked about moving, the more upset I got.

Kevin sensed my frustration. "Well, it's not a straight one, Skids, that's for sure. This kick has some swerve." He stared off into space along with me.

"What?" Swerve was something a soccer player did to make a ball curve through the air. What did that have to do with me moving to Brazil? What the heck was Bones talking about? I wished I hadn't mentioned this to him.

"Life, Skids." Kevin continued. "You moving to Brazil, my mom dying of cancer last year—life will put some swerve on the ball, you know?"

Our eyes met, I knew now that he was the perfect person to speak to about this. "Swerve balls?"

"Yeah, swerve balls, Skids. You'll be fine." He stood up and bumped my knuckle. "You can kick with swerve can't you?" He then took the last sip of his soda and started walking away. He turned to face me. "This is kind of good news."

"Why is that?" I asked.

"Well, I always wanted to go to Africa. Now I have a reason to."

I laughed. "Brazil's in South America, you moron."

"I know, just testing to see if you did." He

shouted. "Swerve balls, Skids!"

I yelled back, "Swerve balls!" And watched Bones disappear.

I sat back on the bench and looked up at the first stars of the night. Kevin was right. Brazil was a kick with swerve—something I hadn't expected. How was I going to handle it? I had no clue. I'd spent most of the past year adjusting to high school. I'd just made the varsity soccer team as a freshman. Everything was going well—until today. I tossed my empty soda into the trash can. Slowly, I dribbled back home.

I opened the door to our house and rounded the corner into the kitchen. Dad was waiting for me. I could tell that he wasn't happy. *Good*, I thought, *that makes two of us.*

"Jason," he started in, "I know this is hard for you. But I expected you to handle this with more maturity."

"Maturity?" I spoke loudly. "It's not like you're asking me what I think about us moving down the block. You're *telling* me that I'm moving halfway around the world!"

"You haven't even given Brazil a chance." Dad remained calm.

"And I don't want to give it a chance!" I was yelling now. I couldn't remember ever having spoken to my father this way. I shook my head, "I don't want to go."

Dad spoke with a forced smile. "Brazil's a great

place, Jas. I know leaving your friends will be tough. It'll be OK, though. Your friends are still your friends no matter where you are. You'll still see them." Dad looked into my eyes and I started to calm down.

"It's not just my friends." I paused, swallowing a lump in my throat. There was a moment of silence that followed. "It's my school, this neighborhood, and my soccer teams. I've worked so hard to get where I am. Do you know how important soccer is to me?"

There was a knowing look in Dad's eyes. "I do, Jas. Trust me, I do."

CHAPTER TWO

CHASING THE KING

Beep. Beep. Beep. I slammed my hand down on the top of my alarm clock. The lights flashed 6:15 A.M. I rolled out of bed. I tried to convince myself that it was a bad dream. I couldn't really be moving to Brazil. I was about to sigh with relief when I glanced over at my desk. I noticed a yellow and green book on top of my soccer jersey. I moved in closer and picked it up. The word Brazil was written across the cover. A short note was written on the inside cover, "Give it a chance." I knew Dad's handwriting from a mile away. It wasn't a dream.

Still, when I threw on my clothes a smile came to my face. I couldn't help smiling. Today was game day, the first of the high school soccer season and my first as a varsity player. I wasn't rusty though. I had been playing soccer all the time with my Bayside United club team. I placed the Brazil book under my left arm and headed downstairs for breakfast.

I passed Dad in the hallway. He followed me down the stairs, asking questions about the game. I answered everything in short sentences. I couldn't help being upset with him. I made my way toward the breakfast table.

When I sat down Dad noticed the book under my arm. "Did you take a look at that yet? You should turn to page thirty. I think you'll like it."

I placed the book down on the table and reached for the newspaper. "I've got a lot of books to read right now." I didn't plan on reading his book any time soon. Besides, I was tired. I'd been awake most of the night. Questions kept popping into my head. I didn't have answers to any of them: *What would life be like? Would I be able to make friends? How would I learn to speak Portuguese? Who would I play soccer with?*

Dad stared across the table at me, then up at Mom. She piled eggs onto my plate. I chewed quietly. Two bagels later, I was heading out the door. I grabbed my soccer bag and left the Brazil book on the table.

School was hard that day. I simply couldn't get our move out of my head. That is, until after school when the whistle blew and our first game started.

Varsity soccer was a completely different game. The stakes were high. People were cheering and booing. The players were enormous. Still, I wasn't intimidated when the ball rolled back to me at midfield. With thoughts of Brazil in my head, I tapped the ball to my left, looking around the field.

From the corner of my eye, I saw Kyle streaking down the right sideline. All I had seen was a blur made by his blue uniform, but I knew it was him. Normally we tried to control the ball with short passes. But if Kyle was sprinting, there was an opportunity.

I quickly moved around a huge opponent and sent a long swerving pass in Kyle's direction. The ball bounced over his head, but he quickly controlled it. Instantly, he was off, dribbling toward the goal box. Kyle flew by the first defender, whose feet looked like they were stuck in concrete. The second defender's slide tackle didn't work either. Kyle calmly flipped the ball over his leg and unleashed a perfect shot. From twenty feet out, the ball bent past the goalie and into the corner of the net. Our teammates mobbed around Kyle in celebration. The small crowd roared. I watched my friend lower his head and jog back to the midline. His face showed no emotion.

We went on to win by a score of three to zero. Kyle was the leader of the freshman soccer players. Having him there made it easier for the rest of us. Even though Kyle was a freshman, he was probably the best player at Hilltop. Everything came naturally to him on the soccer field. Truthfully, if it hadn't been for Kyle, I probably wouldn't have been playing on varsity.

I didn't like Kyle when we first met as teammates in youth soccer at the age of six. He was quiet. He didn't pass. And he scored too much. I remember explaining this to my parents after the last game of our season. The next weekend, Kyle invited me to play miniature golf. After that, our problems were history.

We both grew up in San Francisco but went to different elementary schools. Even though we didn't see each other a lot, our paths did cross through soccer. Like the time I ran into him at Golden Gate Park. We were both twelve at the time and were looking forward to the Bayside United tryouts later that week. "You think any of us twelve-year-olds have a chance of making the team?" I asked Kyle. The team was an under-fourteen group. This meant the competition was open to twelve *and* thirteen-year-olds.

"Maybe," Kyle responded. "But it won't be easy."

A voice rang out from nowhere. "You're right about that. You two have no chance." We both turned and saw Greg Neville and Larry Greenman. They were passing a soccer ball between them. Neville was doing the talking. Both he and Greenman were returning thirteen-year-old players.

"Shut up, Neville." I could feel a fire inside me starting to burn.

Kyle must have noticed, because I felt his hand on my shoulder. "Easy, Skids."

"Scrawny little Skidder. You need your friend

to stick up for you. I take it back. Kyle, you're quick, you have a chance to make it. But your friend here is a joke," Neville smiled an ugly smile.

"How about a friendly game of two-on-two, Greg," Kyle pulled me back. "Short field, narrow goals, no keepers. Skids and I versus you and Larry."

Kyle wasted no time, clearing a small field. We laid down our shirts as goals and walked to meet Greg and Larry. Without saying a word, Greg tossed the ball high into the air between the four of us. Game on. Larry quickly flicked a short pass to Greg. I went for the steal, but missed badly. Greg dribbled the ball into the goal for a one-zero lead.

"One-nothing, Bayside United." Greg yelled as he jogged back on defense.

Kyle's eyes widened as Greg slowly got back. He passed me the ball on the right side. I turned up the field. Neville ran hard to challenge me. He arrived late, gasping for air. The ball was right in front of me. Neville was blocking my lane so I faked a big kick directly at him. He turned, closing his eyes. I guess he wasn't so tough. I laughed loud enough for him to hear me. Then I dribbled and split the goal right down the middle.

The game took on a frantic pace with quick passes and even quicker attacks. Goals went back and forth evenly. After about fifteen minutes, we knew we could hang with these guys. We were trailing six to five when I came up behind Greg to challenge him. He turned his back to me, protecting the ball. For a few seconds, he toyed with the ball. The next thing I remember was his elbow smashing my nose. I hit the ground hard as blood poured out from both nostrils. I looked up and saw Neville and Larry score.

A woman having a picnic handed me a napkin. "Thank you," I said. I placed it on my nose and leaned my head back.

"Seven to five," Neville said, stepping over me on his way back. "Oh, and sorry about that, Skids. Accident, I promise." Neville winked at Larry.

I caught the wink and was more upset than ever. He'd elbowed me on purpose!

"You OK?" Kyle asked.

I tossed the bloody napkin into a nearby garbage can and looked over at Neville. "I'm fine," I said with confidence.

Kyle sensed my will to win. "Lets do this, Skids."

What followed was a battle. The score went back and forth. Neither team gave an inch. We had a chance to win when Kyle was able to steal a pass from Greg. Our opponents fell back on defense as Kyle gave me a sharp pass on the wing. Greg stepped forward to challenge me, but came too fast. I popped a quick ball to Kyle and slipped toward the goal. Kyle gave me a perfect pass. I was able to control the ball in stride and put it through the shirts. Greg and Larry looked on helplessly.

Drenched in sweat, I walked over to Kyle and gave him a tired high five. "Nice ball." Neville stormed off. Larry was a good sport and came over to us. "Nice game guys. I'm looking forward to playing *with* you instead of against you this year. Now go clean up that nose before I puke, Skids." He laughed and gave us both knuckle bumps. I looked over at Kyle. We'd earned our respect. More importantly, our friendship had been cemented.

After that game, Kyle and I sat at a picnic table and ate two giant cheeseburgers. With our faces stuffed, Kyle and I had a conversation that changed my life.

I had thought about playing basketball next season instead of soccer. But I wasn't sure. I knew Kyle was a great point guard and I was curious what his plans were. "Are you going to play basketball this season?"

Kyle's answer was more like a speech. "No, soccer's my sport. It's the greatest game in the world, Skids." He put down his burger and sat up straight. "The field is enormous, you know? And the players are such amazing athletes. You need to have great touch to pass, a soft forehead for headers, and a big foot for corners and goal kicks. You need veins of ice for penalty kicks. Basketball's great, but I want to be a pro in soccer someday. I've got to focus on it. You never know, maybe I can play for Team U.S.A. Maybe we both could." That was the greatest idea I'd ever heard.

I always loved soccer and could never really explain why. But the way Kyle talked about it made sense to me. I wanted to hear more. "What is it that's so great about soccer, Kyle?"

He wiped his mustard-covered face clean. "I just love the idea of chasing the king," he replied. I was silent as he tied his shoelaces into triple knots.

"Huh?" I said

"Do you remember Lazaro's speech last year?" Lazaro was an assistant coach of ours. He was from Italy, where he played professionally.

"Not really Kyle. I couldn't understand his accent. I remember him rambling on about chess or something."

"Chess was his metaphor. But he was talking about soccer." Kyle was really into this. "I don't remember his exact words. He talked about how most sports were like games of chess. Players take out pawns and other less-valued pieces. But soccer's different. It involves wearing your opponent down. In soccer, you're looking for the big victory—your opponent's king. "

"Chasing the king. I like that." I repeated to myself.

"Don't get me wrong, basketball is a great game. The stakes just aren't as high. A single basket isn't that important. But in soccer, every game is close. When you're chasing the king, every game can be turned in a moment. So *every* moment is the most important one of the game!"

I thought about this for a second, "That's true!" I picked up my burger and stared at it. Right then and there, I decided that I wanted to play soccer for a living too. I was twelve and I didn't know much about life. Now there was one thing I *was* sure of. More than anything else, I wanted to be a soccer player. The odds were stacked against me, but I didn't care.

After that conversation, I started playing soccer like it was my job. In fact, Kyle and I spent the next few years practicing every day. We made the Hilltop High varsity team as freshmen.

That first game of the season couldn't have gone any better. Kyle scored twice and I assisted on both goals. Coach Hansen told the entire team about how proud he was of how his freshmen played. It was a great day. But I still had to go home to my parents. I had to go home to the reality of Brazil. I was going to have to chase the king alone.

I avoided speaking to Mom and Dad that night. After dinner I finished my homework and went to my room. The Brazil book sat open-faced on my pillow. I looked through it for awhile. Brazil did have some pretty beaches. *So what?* And the people did seem crazy about soccer. At least that was good. I hoped the kids in Brazil played the way we did in America.

I closed the book at midnight. When I awoke

the next morning, I had a plan. I was going to deal with Brazil my way. So I made an agreement with my parents. They were to let me finish the last four months of my freshman year. I was going to play in the Florida Cup with Bayside United, too. Then, I would move to Brazil with no complaints. Mom and Dad agreed.

Dad moved down three weeks later. Mom, Keri, and I made plans to leave after the Florida Cup. I circled the date on my calendar, hoping it would never come.

CHAPTER THREE

GO FOR IT

It had been two weeks since Dad left. We'd barely spoken since. When he'd call I'd jump in the shower or say I was too tired to talk. Mom did her best to keep us together. She told me about Dad's job in Rio and told Dad about my soccer games. Still, there was a crack in our relationship.

Everywhere I went, Brazil haunted me. At the supermarket, Brazilian style rice was on sale. I turned the television on and a Brazilian team was playing a soccer game. There were magazines and books about Brazil covering our living room table. Brazilian music blasted from the speakers in my sister's room. Every night, Mom and Keri would listen to Portuguese language tapes. They even started speaking to each other in this foreign language. My baby sister was speaking Portuguese!

Feeling comfortable is a big part of being happy. Dad was gone and Mom and Keri were Brazil-crazy. This left only one place where I felt comfortable—the soccer field. Even there, though, it took half the season before our Hilltop team got comfortable playing together. When it happened though, the difference was night and day.

After starting the season with five wins and five losses, we won six in a row to close out the year. That was good enough for a second-place finish in our league. First place belonged to our bitter rivals, West Mission High.

The section tournament began a few days later. We won our first two games easily. Goals were flowing and our defense was solid. The final game would be against West Mission High. We'd already played them twice, so we knew them pretty well.

With a championship at stake, the bus ride down was quiet. I sat in the first row, starting out the window. Coach Hansen approached me, "Mind if I sit, Jason?"

I shook my head and scooted over.

"You ready?" Coach asked without hesitation.

"I guess," I shrugged my shoulders slightly.

"You can't guess. A leader has to know." His eyes grew wide. "Jason," Coach's expression changed.

I sat upright in my seat. "Yeah, Coach."

"I want to say something to you. I know you're

leaving us soon. But you need to hear this first." He looked me in the eyes. "You're as good as anyone on this team. You know that, don't you?" His look was intense and real. "You have great talent. But if you don't have the guts to go for it," he paused, "it's wasted. I just want you to know how much I believe in you."

"Thank you, Coach." I got the chills as Coach got up and left. His speech gave me great confidence heading into the game.

Thirty minutes later, we were facing off against the Bulldogs from West Mission High. They'd pounded us both times we'd played during the regular season. The losses were extra hard on those of us who were also members of Bayside United. The West Mission squad had its freshman talent from Bayside. This list included Rodger Harwell, Greg Neville, Larry Greenman, and my friend Kevin "Bones" Hoover. After each of our losses in the high school games, we had to listen to their bragging.

Kyle and I vowed to turn the tables on them this time. "It's your last high school game in the states. We're going to send you off a champion." Kyle and I bumped knuckles.

Once play started, however, West Mission was killing us. They sliced up our defense like a Thanksgiving turkey. Neville scored on Hamcole, our goalie, one minute into the game. I played OK at midfield, but never had a chance on goal. I was always chasing someone up the sidelines. Their quick strikers were on the attack. Thinking about offense was nearly impossible. When the halftime whistle blew, a sense of relief came over us. We were down one to zero. It could have been worse.

Little was said at halftime as we sipped our water. One goal down to any other team wouldn't have gotten us as worried. But with Bones in goal, we knew we were in trouble. Coming into the section final, he was allowing less than a goal per game. Scoring on him once wasn't going to be easy, let alone twice.

When we took the field in the second half we were fired up. But just five minutes into the game, Rodger Harwell landed a knockout punch. He worked the ball through our defense easily. He reached back and sent a shot toward the right corner of the goal. Hamcole gave a nice effort, but the ball was beyond his reach. Two-nothing, West Mission. We looked like zombies.

This was about to be a horrible ending to my last season. I couldn't let this happen. The referee carried the ball back toward midfield. I raised my hand. "Everyone over here," I yelled. To my surprise, all of my teammates sprinted over. They formed a circle around me.

I spoke with force. "We've got forty minutes left. We need to decide right now if we want to win it. We can't continue with this tomfoolery. I didn't come out here today..." I stopped when I looked around at my teammate's faces. They were all smiling. "What?" I asked. I looked at Kyle, who couldn't stop himself from laughing. *Did I just say "tomfoolery?"*

Marc Stevens, our center midfielder, spoke through a tight grin. "Skids is right, this tomfoolery has gone too far. By golly, let's start playing soccer."

"Gee whiz, guys, this is the playoffs," Nick Goldfarb joked. Everyone broke into laughter. "Skids, are you even from this decade?"

"He may be a nerd," Kyle laughed, "but he's right." He got serious. "Let's play like we know we can." There was a collective "LET'S WIN" and we broke from the circle.

Less than a minute later, we scored an incredible goal. West Mission was pressing forward, looking to put the game out of reach. Harwell danced around two of our defenders. He chipped a perfect pass to a Bulldog striker. Hamcole read the play. He sprinted forward to grab the ball before West Mission's striker got there. They barely missed each other.

I hadn't seen any of this, though. The moment I noticed our goalie rushing forward, I took off. I ran full speed in the opposite direction, hoping to catch West Mission sleeping. Hamcole heaved a beautiful line drive to my feet and I was able to control it. With a running start, I dribbled around the first West Mission defender. Behind me, I saw the blur of Kyle's blond hair. I also noticed two more defenders sprinting into position.

I dribbled toward the center of the field to draw the crowd. Just before the ball was taken from me, I passed it off to Kyle. He slowed up and started to put a move on the defender. Then he backed away. I was running toward the right edge of the goal. Kyle quickly flipped the ball into the air. On the short hop, he pounded a shot toward the right goalpost. Bones dove and made a great save, but the rebound came to me. Before he could pounce again, I one-timed a laser. I smiled as I watched the back net ripple.

We'd scored! I'd scored! I ran over to the corner and was surrounded by my teammates. We jogged back to midfield to restart play..

Somehow, we put two more balls past Bones to take a three to two lead. West Mission tried everything in the last few minutes. The game took on a lightning fast pace. With ten Bulldogs pushing forward at every chance, they were getting off a lot of shots.

Time was winding down when West Mission had another corner kick. "Goldfarb, get on number ten." Hamcole barked instructions as we gathered inside the penalty box.

"You want me leaving the post?" This was a fair question from Goldfarb. He had been assigned the right post for most of the year.

"Get on ten, Goldfarb. Don't let him out-jump you," Hamcole hissed back. "Skids, right post."

"Sure," I jogged to the goal line.

The West Mission player taking the corner kick was delaying. At first I didn't understand why, especially since they needed to hurry. Then I saw Bones in a full sprint coming to join the action. Pulling the goalie for offense is almost never done in soccer. Time was running out and West Mission was desperate. Bones jogged into our box.

"Hart, mark color boy," Hamcole said, pointing to Bones's colorful goalie jersey. Just then, a high-arching corner kick swerved toward the center of the box. A few players fought for position. Others took a final step and jumped into the air. Goldfarb out-jumped number ten. I thought he would win the ball. But from out of nowhere, I watched Bones rise above the crowd. With a snap of his neck, he headed the ball directly at me near the right post.

I didn't have a split second to think. I jumped and tried to deflect it with my head. I felt the ball skim the top of my hair. I looked back, expecting to see it in our net. Instead, it bounced left of the goal. Somehow, I'd changed its course. The ball rolled away from the field and a West Mission player sprinted after it. A second later, the whistle blew, ending the game.

We were section champs! I clenched my fists and my teammates ran over to me. There was a massive dog pile and I was at the bottom.

Afterward, in our locker room meeting, Coach Hansen gave me the game ball. He let me know how much I would be missed next season, too. My teammates all wished me luck in Brazil. I thanked them all.

Just before I left the locker room Coach Hansen tapped me on the shoulder. "See what happens when you go for it?"

CHAPTER FOUR

A NEW FRIEND

I picked up the phone, "Hello?"

"Jason?"

"Dad?" There was a short silence. It had been over a month since he'd left and this was one of our first talks. "How are you?" I asked.

"I'm good, you?"

"Good." I paused, trying to think of something to say. "Mom says you like your job…that's good."

"Yeah, and she said you guys won the section, congratulations."

"It was great, Dad," I smiled.

"I wish I could have been there." He paused, "It's good to hear your voice, Jason."

"You too," I said. I went on to give Dad an account of the game.

"Incredible Jas. Sounds like this turned out to

be a great soccer year. And with that Bayside tourney in Florida, it could get even better."

"Yeah, we've been playing pretty well. We'll see what happens. I was actually just packing my bag when I heard the phone." I paused, we still hadn't talked about Brazil. "So how's Brazil?"

I could tell Dad was smiling. "It's great, thanks for asking."

This felt a weird. I repeated my comment from earlier, "And you said you like your job, so that's good."

"Yeah, work has been going well. My Portuguese stinks, though. It's beautiful down here, Jas. Did Mom tell you that I found a house?" Dad went on talking about our new house. I wasn't really listening. The move to Brazil was suddenly too real. June 26 was only a few weeks away. Sad feelings of leaving everything and everyone popped into my head. No more penalty shots in the park with Bones. No more pizza parties with the Hilltop team. No more anything as far as I was concerned.

Dad woke me from my trance, "Well?"

I was confused, "Yeah Dad, sounds great."

"What sounds great, Jas? I asked you how math was coming?"

"Sorry. Good. I aced my last test and I think I've got a B." My voice was shaking.

"You OK, son?"

I wanted to let Dad in on how I was feeling.

"Actually, I'm pretty scared, Dad."

Dad cleared his throat, "I know that, Jas. And I'm proud of the way you've handled yourself. Don't worry. The Brazilians are great. Just promise me you'll come with an open mind."

Hearing Dad's words made me want to cry for some reason. But I didn't. I had to get off the phone. "I'll see you soon, Dad." I quickly handed the phone to my mother. I ran upstairs to pack for Florida.

Twenty-four hours later, I was on an overnight flight from San Francisco to Miami. Kyle was in the window seat to my left. On my right, Jeremy Vint had fallen into a light sleep. Across the way, Neville, Goldfarb, and Harwell were playing cards. Before I knew it, the five-hour flight was over.

Our first game wasn't for three days. So when we got to Miami we had an off day. As long as we were back at the hotel by 7:00 P.M. for dinner we could do as we pleased. Kyle and I were in our shorts right away. We were on the beach by noon. We rented surfboards and hung out on the white beaches under the Florida sun.

I was daydreaming about Brazil when a voice rang out from above me. "This is the guy I was telling you about." Nick Goldfarb stood above me with a girl he'd met that afternoon. I wasn't surprised. Girls always seemed to like hanging out with Nick. "Skids, meet Mariana. She's from Brazil. You're moving to

Brazil. You guys should be friends." That seemed simple enough.

I rolled over and popped to my feet. The sun was shining in my eyes as I looked up. I was staring at a beautiful, dark-skinned, dark-haired, dark-eyed, dark-everything girl. She was wearing a green bikini and a pair of green sunglasses. I had never seen a girl this pretty in my life. Not on television, not in a magazine, not even in my dreams. I think I said hello. I think I waved my hand. I'm not one hundred percent sure, though. I may have just stared at her.

A few of her friends ran into the water with Kyle and Bones. Nick quickly followed, leaving me alone with her. Talking with girls was never my greatest skill. She spoke in a thick accent. "Nick thinks that because you are moving to Brazil, you will bump into me. He speaks like Brazil is a small town. We are the fifth largest country in the world." She giggled, "I'm sorry, I talk a lot when I'm nervous."

I responded quickly, "No, I'm sorry, I don't say anything when *I'm* nervous."

"Skids, your name is Skids?" I nodded and we shook hands. "I am Mariana. Skids, voce fala português?"

"Ummmm…I think you just asked me if I speak Portuguese. The answer is no. Not yet," I responded.

"But you understood me very well. You'll be fine learning Portuguese." She sat down next to me on my towel. "So, where exactly are you moving in

Brazil?" she asked.

For some reason, I was comfortable with Mariana. I spoke truthfully. "To be honest, I know nothing about Brazil. My father took a job in Rio. He's already down there. The rest of my family will be joining him in two weeks."

"Rio? Well, your father chose the best city in the world. I live just outside of Rio. How do you call this in English?"

I thought for a second, "A suburb?"

"That's it," she smiled, pleased with my quick thinking. "So, we will be neighbors. And we probably *will* bump into one another."

"That's great." I couldn't think of anyone I'd rather bump into. I smiled at her and got the courage to say. "You'll be the prettiest neighbor I've ever had."

She blushed. "Thank you, Skids." The mood changed for a second. I was sure that my comment had embarrassed her. "So I'll be back home in about a week. If you need a guide or if you want to go to the beach or something, e-mail me." She tore a piece of paper from inside her handbag and scribbled an e-mail address onto it.

"Thanks," I said, placing the piece of paper in my wallet. Now I knew a local Brazilian before I even got down there. And she had to be the nicest one in the entire country. Way to go Goldfarb! "I'll catch up with you in a few weeks then." I spoke in the deepest voice I could.

"Well, Nick actually invited us to come watch your team play. Maybe I'll see you sooner than that." With that, she got up and left. I couldn't stop smiling as she walked back over to her friends.

The next two days passed slowly. I couldn't tell what I was looking forward to more: our first game or seeing Mariana again. As we warmed up for a game against a team from Texas, I scanned the stands for Mariana. I found her taking a seat just before kickoff. She waved and looked at me, flashing a smile. I returned her gaze as I fell back into our passing drills.

Just a goal or two and Mariana would really be impressed with me, I thought. Unfortunately, I never got that opportunity. We were outplayed in a four-zero defeat. Our ball movement was slow and our defense was weak. We were outmatched by our opponents. They were stronger and in better shape than anyone on our team. It was a new feeling for many of us. We were used to being the best.

After the game, our coaches tried to keep our spirits up. The loss, however, meant that we moved into the loser's bracket. We faced an uphill climb to the finals.

For my own part, I played miserably in the Texas game. I turned the ball over about five times. Afterward, I was angry at myself for getting sidetracked by Mariana and my hopes of scoring a goal. Soccer is a team game, not a one-man show. I avoided seeing her after the game. Instead, I turned my thoughts to our next opponent.

With our backs against the wall, we responded the next morning with a two-one win over West Virginia. That same afternoon, we earned a three to one win over our rivals from Southern California. That set up a match with the Red Devils from Oklahoma. The Devils were feared by everyone. This was not because of their soccer skills. It was because of their reputation as a dirty team. They scratched, clawed, and bit their way to victory. Giving them much of this image was a guy named Rube Jones. Rube was the biggest and toughest fifteen-year-old on the planet! He was over six feet tall and probably weighed about 230 pounds. His head was shaved near bald and his neck was as thick as my thigh.

Oklahoma jumped out to an early one-zero lead. That allowed them to play a defensive game. While trying to find a goal, we took a number of hard hits from their players. Vint had to leave the game after a flying elbow bloodied his nose. Greenman had the wind knocked out of him. The real blow, however, came late in the first half. It came at the hands, or rather the feet, of big Rube Jones.

Kyle was streaking up the right sideline. He was looking for an opportunity to cross the ball. From nowhere, Rube came at him with cleats up. In trying a slide tackle from behind, Rube's cleats smashed Kyle's ankle. He went down with a scream and rolled over three times. Kyle had a pained look on his face and was forced to leave the game. He would be in a cast and on crutches the next day. Doctors later called it a "clean break." I didn't see anything clean about it.

I was mad when I turned to face Rube, who had just received a red card. "You're a joke, you know that," I looked up at the giant fifteen-year-old. "Go home. Get off the field."

"Easy number four," the ref turned away from Rube and stared at me.

I backed away. The last thing our team needed was for me to get into trouble. The red card meant Rube was ejected from the game. The Red Devils would have to finish with ten players, instead of the usual eleven. Having one more player than our opponent helped us turn the tide of the game. We attacked their goal for the rest of the afternoon. Harwell scored twice and Neville got his first of the year. We smashed a Rube-less Oklahoma team, three to one. We'd crawled our way back to the winner's bracket. We faced the hometown, Miami Power Club, for the chance to play in the finals.

I was leaving the field when I heard Mariana's voice from the stands, "Skids!"

I looked up and she was waving at me. I waved back and made my way over to her in the bleachers. "You came," I said smiling.

"Of course. That was some *futebol* out there."

"Yeah, tell me about it. Those guys should be

wearing helmets and scoring touchdowns." I agreed, those Oklahoma guys were playing the wrong sport.

She laughed because I'd misunderstood her. "Not that football, Skids. My futebol—your soccer. In Brazil, we call soccer "futebol." But you're right, those guys were pretty rough out there."

"A little too rough, if you ask me."

"Well, you'll have to make more runs from midfield. With Kyle out, you'll need to be aggressive. You've got good team speed. Your fullbacks should be able to cover any holes you might leave on the attack." *Man, this girl knew her soccer!*

I couldn't have said it better myself. "Sounds like good advice, coach. How do you know so much about the game?" I asked.

"Oh, I've picked up a thing here and there," she laughed. "Skids, you'll be surprised at how important futebol is in Brazil. We can talk more about that later. I'll let you run. I know you've got to get ready for tomorrow."

Even with the soothing sound of the ocean outside our hotel, it was difficult to sleep. We would face Miami in the morning. If we won, we'd play the championship game that night. I thought about the game, of Mariana, and of what Coach Hansen said to me about going for it. These were good, happy thoughts, but they still kept me up all night. When the sunlight finally crept through the curtains, I wasn't sure if I'd slept a wink.

The 8:00 A.M. kickoff didn't keep the Miami Power Club fans away from the game. I felt light-headed when we started. This was probably a result of my lack of sleep. Once that whistle blew, I was fine.

The crowd's energy kept Miami in the game early. But after a few minutes it was clear that we were the better squad. We controlled the tempo and the ball for most of the game. I scored a goal and we got two more from Vint. Bones earned his first shutout of the tournament.

With the championship game that evening, we never left the field that day. We tried to take our minds off soccer, but that proved impossible. The championship game was a rematch against Texas. Their defense hadn't allowed a goal yet, meaning we would need a special offensive game. With Kyle out, who was this special game going to come from?

By 6:00 P.M., the lights went on and the stadium began to fill. We'd done enough thinking—it was time to play.

As expected, Texas came out looking strong. They controlled the ball and the game for most of the first half. Luckily, Bones was able to deflect or catch every shot on goal. He single-handedly kept us in the game. Our offense, on the other hand, looked awful. Without Kyle, we hadn't put any pressure on the Texas goalie.

At halftime, our coaches talked strategy. The question on everyone's mind was how to penetrate the Texas defense. "Coach, I'm just not sure how we can get through. They're bigger and faster than us." Larry Greenman's comment sounded gloomy. What was worse was that everyone agreed with him.

Our head coach took a deep breath. He was about to speak, but I did first. "I agree with you, Larry. If Harwell and I push forward on offense, it opens our defense. But I didn't come all the way out to Florida to tie in the championship game.."

"What are you getting at Skids?" Coach asked.

"Well, say Harwell and I do push forward on offense. We'll need to know that our defense will come forward to fill the holes we leave. I won't stop running until that whistle blows." My confidence was fueled by the words of my high school coach, Coach Hansen. His comments changed my attitude about soccer.

"I like the idea, Skids. But you guys will run out of gas in this heat."

"Let us worry about that, Coach. If either of us falls over, sub us out." I looked over at Harwell. He supported my plan.

Coach saw the fire burning in my eyes. "OK then," he nodded. "Harwell, you and Skids press forward. Larry, hang back and roam the midfield. You defenders will have to be aggressive, come up and challenge. Bones, this'll leave you unprotected at times."

"I can handle it." Bones was all business.

"All right then, let's get out there and beat us some Texans!" Coach loved that line, "beat us some." He said it no matter who we were playing.

The second half began and our strategy backfired. With Harwell and I pushing forward, we moved into the Texas half of the field. But a poor pass gave Texas the ball back. They were heading the other way quickly. One of the Texan midfielders dribbled freely. Harwell and I sprinted back to stop him. We both arrived too late. He had time to pick his spot. He reared back and nailed a shot toward the upper right corner of the goal. I was sure this one was in. But Bones stepped up. With outstretched arms, he knocked the ball over the post. I was out of breath, trying to suck in more humid air. I was sure glad Bones was on our team.

The game went back and forth. Both teams tested their physical limits in the hot and sticky Florida air. The score remained zero to zero as we searched for scoring chances. One finally came with three minutes left. Harwell dribbled through the Texas defense and was tripped ten feet outside the penalty box. This set up a free kick for our team. Normally, Kyle would handle the free kicks. He had the best swerve of anyone on our team. But without him, the task fell to either Harwell or myself.

I looked over at Harwell. "Take it, Skids," he

said. He jogged down into the box for the chance to score on a rebound. I bent down and set the ball in position. *Concentrate Jason*, I thought to myself. I took a few steps behind the ball. Texas quickly set up a wall, blocking the goal. I watched the wall grow as players added themselves to it. I checked the goalie's position for signs of weakness. My eyes caught a small flaw on the right side. The post was guarded by the shortest player on the field. *Put it over his head Jas. You can do it*. I closed my eyes and visualized the flight of the ball.

The ref's whistle woke me and I started toward the ball. Three steps. Head down. Left foot—plant. *Boom!* I hammered the ball with all my force. Everything was in slow motion. I watched as the ball curled over the wall of players, just as I'd aimed. I had put some serious swerve on the ball. It danced sideways toward the right corner of the net. The keeper dove left and managed to get a finger on the ball. It wasn't enough. The force of my shot blew by him into the goal.

One-zero, Bayside! Harwell, Goldfarb and Greenman swarmed me. I tried to stay calm. No celebrations before that final whistle blew. Still, it was impossible not to smile.

Three minutes still remained. I knew that Texas would bring everyone up to try and tie the score. The rest of that game was the fastest, toughest soccer I'd ever been a part of. Texas chipped balls into the center hoping for a lucky bounce. They elbowed for position and pushed to clear space. They unleashed perfect shots and Bones made amazing saves.

Neither team scored again. I raised my arms as the whistle blew, crowning Bayside the champions. The celebration on the field was short. The tournament organizers hurried to set up the awards ceremony. I was shocked when I made the all-tournament team along with Bones. There was no time to enjoy the feeling. Our flight back to California was in a few hours. And my flight to Brazil was scheduled for the following morning.

Coach apologized for us having to leave so quickly and then screamed, "Two minutes to be on the bus. Hustle!"

I threw my sweaty jersey and socks into my sports bag and jogged to the bus. Then I heard Mariana's voice. "Skids, no goodbye?"

"Mariana!" I turned and saw her running up to catch me. "I'm sorry but we've got to catch this flight. I've got your e-mail address, I'll write you as soon as I get to Braz..." I felt a hand on my shoulder.

It was Coach. "Skids, that goal earned you three extra minutes." He looked down and started the timer on his watch. "Three minutes. No more, or we'll head back to California without you." He smiled at me.

"Thanks Coach," I said, turning back to Mariana. "So I guess I'll write you when I get down there."

"You won't forget, will you?" she said.

"It'll be the first thing I do. It's not like I've got any other friends down there." I wished I could have taken that line back. "What I mean is that—"

She smiled and put her finger to my lips, "Shhh." She removed a necklace she was wearing and put it on me. It was made out of beads. "Now there's no way you can forget your Brazilian friend."

"Wow, it's really nice." I looked down at the first piece of jewelry I'd ever worn. I was definitely going to be teased for this when I got on the bus. Looking at Mariana, I didn't care. "I feel bad. I've got nothing for you." I thought hard for a second, "unless you'd like a shin guard."

"No thank you," she held her nose. "I'll let you keep those."

I looked down at the all-tournament medal I was holding in my hand. It was the greatest prize I had ever won. Without hesitation I handed it to her. "Take this," I said.

But she wouldn't accept it. "That's yours, you earned it. Just smile for me Skids," she said.

"What?" I asked, and smiled at the same time.

"I'll remember you, Skids."

"You can call me Jason, that's my real name. I mean, if you want to."

"OK—Jason."

"Skidder!" it was coach. My three minutes were up. Mariana knew it too and she held her hand up for a high five. I gave her one, but instead of slapping my hand she squeezed it. "I'll be waiting to hear from you." She reached up, pecked a kiss onto my cheek, and headed off. I stood wondering what in the heck had just happened. Whatever it was, I decided that today was the greatest day of my life.

A voice shouted from the bus window. "See you in California, Skidder." I turned and ran. When I stepped onto the bus, I was greeted in typical fashion. There were whistles and lines like "Hey, lover boy" and "nice necklace, cutie pie." None of it bothered me. I felt like I was walking on air.

I took a seat on my own in the back of the bus and stared out the window. It was dusk and the passing trees were barely visible. Lightning crackled in the distance. A gentle rain began to fall. All I could think about was the sun shining on my life lately. *High school champs with Hilltop. Tournament champs with Bayside. A goal in both championship games! The all-tournament team! And Mariana!* These thoughts kept replaying in my head. Then a new thought brought a smile to my face: *Bring on Brazil, I can handle anything right now.*

CHAPTER FIVE

RIO

"Last call for flight 1226 to Rio de Janeiro," a woman's voice boomed over the airport intercom.

"That's me." My heart raced. "I'm really leaving." I turned and faced Kyle, who was still on crutches.

"Don't worry, Skids, you'll be fine. From everything I hear, you're headed to a cool place." Kyle handed me five soccer magazines, "for the plane ride."

"Thanks, Kyle." I paused. "You'll come down to visit, right?"

"Of course we will. Bones, Harwell, Goldfarb—we'll even bring Neville down." Kyle and I smiled. He held out his hand. I grabbed it and slapped his back in a hug. I wondered when the next time we'd see each other would be. I wondered if this was the beginning of the end of our friendship.

I walked down toward the entrance to the plane, shooting Kyle one last wave. "Keep chasing the king!"

he yelled as I turned the corner and disappeared.

Fifteen minutes later I buckled my seat belt and leaned my head against the window. I watched San Francisco get smaller and smaller until it disappeared. I'd been staring down this tidal wave for four months now. As we soared to ten thousand feet, I felt it crash over me. I put my head between my hands.

"What a mope," my seven-year-old sister called out from the seat next to me. "We get to go to Brazil, to a new house, and a new…"

Mom cut Keri off, "Leave your brother alone." She understood what I was going through. Mom's voice was firm and Keri was quiet the rest of the flight.

I spent most of the next thirteen hours staring out the window. I wondered what would be in store for me when we touched ground in Rio. We passed over the Gulf of Mexico and then the Atlantic Ocean. It was a really long day of flying. The last few hours went quickly, though. I buried my head in the pile of soccer magazines that Kyle had given me.

I was really into this one article when my sister's hand shot across my seat. She pointed out the window. "There it is! Rio de Janeiro! It's just like the pictures, Jason."

I looked out the window. Even though I was feeling nervous, I couldn't help cracking a smile. The Rio skyline was unlike anything I'd ever seen. I'd been told it was one of the natural wonders of the world, and now I understood why. Massive green hills shot up all around the city. Colorful houses and buildings stood wherever there was flat land near the water. With all the hills jutting upward, the city was set away from the beaches. This left the coast more natural-looking.

"Welcome to Rio de Janeiro," the pilot's voice crackled. "I hope each of you enjoys your visit." *So do I*, I thought to myself. Except this wasn't just a visit.

When we arrived at the gate, Dad was waiting with open arms. He looked so excited. My sister ran over to give him a hug, followed by Mom. I could feel his eyes on me the entire time. Finally, I approached him and smiled. "It's beautiful, Dad." I gave him a hug and started to pull away. His grip was too tight to escape. He kept hugging me for another second and then went to help with our bags. As he released me, I released some of my anger toward him. I still didn't understand why he moved us here. Someday I hoped to. But today we arrived in Brazil—and that was that.

Needless to say, we had a ton of luggage. Each of us had packed three large suitcases, not to mention all the stuff Mom had shipped. We jumped into a yellow jeep and left the airport. "What do you think of the car?" Dad smiled. I was sure Mom would yell at him. She never liked bright cars.

To my surprise, Mom kissed Dad on the cheek. "I love it," she said.

Dad was like a tour guide, pointing out everything we passed. He told us our new home was only fifteen minutes from the airport. After about ten minutes, I realized we were driving through my new neighborhood. I wondered where Mariana lived. More than anything, though, I wondered what was with my Dad? He was wearing dark sunglasses and his shirt was covered with pink flowers. And he wouldn't stop smiling! Did I mention the fact that he was driving a yellow jeep? Who was this guy?

I hadn't done much talking all day. I glanced out the window and spoke my first words about Rio. "Lots of fruit juice stands, huh Dad?"

This was my brilliant question, to which Dad responded, "Yeah, I guess."

Mom started laughing. "That's the first thing you've said since San Francisco. You're pretty funny, Jason."

I had to laugh at myself. For the first time in four months, we were a family. We were laughing in a yellow jeep, driving through the streets of Rio. Talk about a kick with some swerve.

A minute later we pulled into a driveway leading to a big house—it was our house. Everyone agreed that Dad had done well picking out our new home. I had no complaints. My bedroom was twice the size of the one in San Francisco. Plus, I had a door that led to our backyard. We had a swimming pool and seven mango trees. I pictured myself lying back on a raft in the pool, eating mangoes in the sun. I could definitely live with that.

After dinner that night, I e-mailed Mariana and received a quick reply. We made plans to meet the following afternoon. I was anxious and lied awake in bed that night. I listened to the sounds of strange birds. Even the wind sounded strange. *Was I really in Brazil?* Just before I fell asleep I wondered what my friends were doing in America. I wondered what they would think of my new home.

The next afternoon I met Mariana for a walking tour of the city. Her older brother lived by our new house, so she knew my neighborhood well. We walked through the busy streets and took the cable car up to the top of Pão de Azucar. In English it means "sugarloaf," and it is one of the massive hills of Rio. On our way home, we walked through a small park. Right away, I noticed soccer games being played. Brazil was definitely soccer country. It was rare to see any pick-up soccer games in America. But in Rio, every park was filled with people kicking around soccer balls. *Now this is beautiful*, I thought to myself.

Mariana and I sat on a bench and watched the games. They were great games. There were heel taps, bicycle kicks, and more swerve than should even be legal. The thing I noticed right away was the fun they had when they played. In America, soccer players are more serious on the field. But in America, they weren't nearly as good as the players I was watching.

I looked at Mariana. "Who are these guys? Are

they some kind of club team?"

She clapped her hands and laughed as one of the players fell to the ground. "No, these are just some guys from the neighborhood."

"They sure can play," I gulped.

"So can you, Jason." She gave me a push, "Get out there."

"I don't know," I said. "I'm real tired from the flight and I don't even have my cleats."

She jumped to her feet and pulled my arm, "Nobody in Brazil plays with cleats." She started yelling out to one of the players. He waved his hand, signaling me into the game. He immediately ran off the field and sat on the grass. Apparently, nobody could say no to Mariana. I had no choice but to head onto the field.

Some of these players were older than me. That was one reason they were better than I was—or that was one excuse I could use anyway! But they weren't just a little bit better than me. They were on a completely different level. They ran around me like I wasn't even there. After a few confusing minutes, I felt as though I didn't know anything about soccer.

Nobody understood me when I shouted phrases like "right here" or "on your left." I guess I sounded funny, because everyone laughed when I spoke. Despite being outmatched, I was having fun.

So everything was fine until I made a small mistake. The guy in the white shorts had stolen the ball and passed it to "yellow shirt," our team's best player. He was probably the best player I'd ever played with. I broke upfield and, to my surprise, "yellow shirt" sent a pass in my direction. I controlled the ball and turned to face the goalkeeper. "Yellow shirt" had also broken forward. With his speed he was blowing past defenders. I was about to pass the ball back to him for what would have been a sure score. At the last second, though, I saw a clear angle on goal. I decided to take the shot. Just as I was about to kick it, the goalie charged. The angle closed and my shot sailed left.

I was upset that I had missed, but this was just a friendly pick-up game. Or so I thought. Next thing I know, "yellow shirt" was in my face, yelling and screaming at me. There was saliva spraying from his mouth. In the middle of all the Portuguese, I heard, "Mariana this" and "Mariana that." Our teammates pulled him back. By this point, Mariana had run over and was yelling back at "yellow shirt." He turned and left me alone, returning to the game.

I walked back to my seat on the park bench, confused. A few guys came up to me and apologized for their friend's behavior. At least I think they were apologizing. I couldn't tell—they were all speaking Portuguese!

Mariana yapped a bit longer at "yellow shirt" and then rejoined me on the sideline. *Great, I've been here less than two days and already I have an en-*

emy. He must have been an old boyfriend of hers. I didn't really care. I waited to see if she wanted to bring it up. She didn't at first, so we sat in silence.

When we finally left the park, Mariana spoke up. "I'm sorry about what happened back there." She looked more embarrassed than anything.

"Don't apologize," I said. "It's not your fault. That guy's just a jerk."

Mariana took my hand in hers and we continued walking.

Brazil was going to take a lot of getting used to. I had no control over my life anymore. For instance, I assumed summer vacations were the same throughout the world. What I hadn't realized was how the seasons were reversed in South America. I left a California summer for a Rio winter. I'd just finished my ninth grade school year at Hillside. Two weeks later, I was beginning tenth grade at the International Education School. And Portuguese was proving to be much harder than I thought it would be. When I tried to speak it, people would laugh in my face. Despite Mariana's tutoring, I couldn't even order a sandwich.

I didn't want to upset anyone. I kept it to myself that I hated Rio. Sure, it has a beautiful landscape and the beaches are great. But the city was too big for me, and too loud. People stared at me because I looked and dressed different.

But my parents were happier than I ever remembered seeing them. I couldn't argue with that. They were walking on the beach and laughing all the time. Keri adjusted to her new surroundings easily too. She instantly made new friends and was speaking Portuguese like a native. My sister was special like that. So I didn't feel too bad when she had her entire class over to swim in our pool. We had been in Brazil for four days.

It took me a lot longer to find my groove in Brazil.

Sitting on a raft in our pool, while Keri's friends swam around me, I daydreamed. The sounds of giggling and shouting in Portuguese faded away. I was no longer there. Instead, I was back in San Francisco. My cleats were laced up and I was running across the Golden Gate Bridge. I was dribbling a soccer ball with Kyle and Bones by my side. Ahead of us, a king wearing a crown on his head was running at full speed. I wasn't alone in Brazil anymore. I was chasing the king with my friends again. And do you know what the best part about this dream was? Every word we spoke to each other was in English.

CHAPTER SIX

ESCAPE

Luckily, I had Mariana in my life. I had never spent so much time with a girl before. We were together nearly every day even though we went to different schools.

My school was filled with international students. Most of my classes were taught in English. Mariana went to public high school. I hoped that next year my Portuguese would be good enough to attend with her.

I'd been in Brazil three weeks and still hadn't touched a soccer ball since that first day. I saw a few kids playing in another park just down the street. I wanted to play, but I wasn't sure how to ask if I could join. So I never did.

Meanwhile, Kyle and Bones were sending me e-mail updates all the time. They talked about Bayside United tournaments and let me know how much the team missed me at midfield. My game-winning goals and our championship just a few weeks ago were distant memories. It looked as if my soccer career was going nowhere. The glow I had come down to Brazil with had faded.

I didn't like being sad. So I was excited when Mariana invited me to go camping with her and her Brazilian friends. She told me not to forget my soccer ball, which made me both nervous and excited. I was ready to start making some friends. We would be spending the weekend camping on the beach of Boisucanga. Eight of us were going on the trip. There was me, Mariana, her girlfriends Paula and Daniella, and the guys—Ricardo, Pablo, Danny, and Patricio.

Due to my lack of confidence in Portuguese, I only felt comfortable speaking in English. This left the other six in our van speaking Portuguese and ignoring me in the back of the van. Or so I thought.

I spoke to Mariana. "This Ricardo guy drives like a maniac. Everyone drives crazy down here, so I guess he's the norm." She glared at me, but I continued. "Why does Paula dye her hair blue? Do all your guy friends have tattoos or just these guys? Who is Daniella's boyfriend because Pablo's been looking at her the entire ride?"

About twenty minutes into a five hour ride, Ricardo turned to me. "Skids, O seu nome é Skids?" He was asking me if my name was Skids.

I had practiced this bit with my language teacher.

I knew how to respond. "Não, meu nome e Jason, mas todo o mundo me chama de Skids." *No, my name is Jason but everyone calls me Skids*, I think is what I said.

"OK, Skids. Você Gosta do Rio...da cidade, do povo?" He'd lost me. I had no idea what he was saying.

I responded with my one trusty line, "Não falo muito Português." This meant *I don't speak much Portuguese.*

"Ahhh, voce fala aquela frase muito bem," Ricardo said. He turned and gave me a big thumbs up. In Brazil the thumbs up can mean anything from "good one" to "thank you."

"What did he say?" I nudged Mariana.

Before Mariana could respond, Ricardo looked at me in the rear view mirror. "I said, 'but you speak that phrase very well.'"

Everyone in the car chuckled. My face turned red. "Does everyone here speak English?" I asked, placing my head in my hands in embarrassment. Judging by their smiles I knew the answer. They'd understood everything I'd said.

Pablo turned around. "I don't have any tattoos and, yes, Daniella is my girlfriend. And I'm pretty sure blue is Paula's favorite color. Am I right?" he spoke in perfect English.

"You are, but also because blue matches my beautiful eyes," Paula replied to Pablo. She was smiling at me. The whole car exploded with laughter. I smiled and slouched in my seat. I was quiet for the rest of the ride.

When we pulled up to our camping spot, we all jumped into the waves. The warm Atlantic Ocean was a perfect spot to stretch our legs after the long car ride. This was the most beautiful beach I had ever stepped foot on. I took a second to appreciate it.

Ricardo ran up to the parked car and grabbed my soccer ball. "Hey Skids, you want to have a kick?"

I was hoping for a chance to redeem myself. "Yeah," I said relieved that he hadn't asked in Portuguese. Soccer was a language that I knew how to speak.

We began juggling the ball and passing it back and forth. The goal was not to let the ball touch the ground. Soon, everyone joined us. I was amazed at their skills. Pablo would stop the ball on his bare foot and flick it over to Daniella. She'd use the outside of her foot to pass to Mariana. Mariana would juggle it effortlessly with both feet and head the ball to someone else. It was the first time I had seen Mariana play. I was impressed.

"Let's get a game of soccer in before the sun goes down," I said as Danny and Patricio began hogging the ball.

"Sounds good. Except for one thing," Ricardo grabbed the ball from Danny and Patricio.

"What's that?"

He leaned in, putting his hand on my shoulder. "The rest of the world uses the word futebol, not soccer. You live in the rest of the world now, so drop the word soccer. It doesn't sound right."

"Cool—futebol," I said grabbing the ball from Ricardo.

He shrugged his shoulders, confused by my slang. "Cool? Is the ball cold?"

I laughed, and left Ricardo standing with a funny look on his face.

A moment later we divided up into teams of four. We played on the hard sand near the water. Mariana told Ricardo that I was a good player. He put me on a team with Patricio, Paula, and Daniella.

The score was quickly thirteen to three. It was clear that the teams were unbalanced. Ricardo and Pablo were dancing around me on every play. I was looking foolish.

Ricardo and I were face to face on one of the last plays of the game. I vowed to stay with him. He faked inside by swinging his leg out and around the ball without touching it. I bit on the fake so hard that my feet got tangled and I lost my balance. I rolled over twice before coming to a stop. I was terrible.

I'd never felt as slow or clumsy as I did on the beach that afternoon. When the sun dipped too low for us to continue, we quit. Everyone but me ran up the beach to start setting up the tents. I sat in the sand and stared at my feet. *What had just happened?*

Mariana noticed that I was upset. She joined me on the sand. "You OK, Jason?"

"No, I'm not." I was always hard on myself when it came to soccer. "That was embarrassing." I grabbed some sand and tossed it.

"What, the car ride? Don't worry about that. They were just having fun."

"Oh yeah, the car ride, I forgot about that. That was embarrassing too. But I was talking about the futebol game. The way I played. I was miserable. I've never in my life..." my voice trailed off. I didn't have anything left to say.

Mariana sat down next to me and let her head fall onto my shoulder. "You're being hard on yourself. You're not used to playing on the beach. You're used to cleats and grass. You'll play better tomorrow."

With Mariana next to me, I wasn't able to stay mad for long. Soon, we were all sitting around a bonfire as Pablo played his guitar. I laid down on my back and gazed upward into the night sky. Here I was on a tiny beach in southern Brazil. I wondered what my friends were doing at this exact moment. I was having a good time, but I couldn't help thinking about them. They were probably off at a movie or playing basketball back in Dolores Park. *Man, I wish I was there.*

Thinking of home got me thinking about soccer. I thought about my horrible performance that afternoon. *You'll play better tomorrow.* I repeated Mariana's words in my head and closed my eyes, listening to the quiet music of the guitar.

I didn't play any better the next day, though. In fact, I might have played worse. Time and time again, I was left in the dust. Ricardo had really quick feet and seemed to enjoy beating me with his footwork. Still, after every goal, he would run back shrugging his shoulders. "Another lucky one," he would say in broken English. Ricardo was the kind of guy that you couldn't get angry at. Even when he made you look silly on the soccer field. Everyone liked him, and I did too.

We must have played six separate games that day. Despite my team losing all but one, everyone was a good sport. They continued to encourage the slow-footed American. Too bad I couldn't find any way to encourage myself. I was having serious doubts about my soccer skills.

When I came down here I knew Brazilians took their soccer seriously. I knew they supported their national team too. But I never thought everyone would be so good at playing the game. I guess I should have known. I would have to learn a lot if I wanted to catch up.

After the ride back to Rio, Ricardo dropped me off outside my house. He turned to me. "Skids, you should come play futebol with us sometime. We play every day down at the Palácio de Maria after school. We've got real goals and goalkeepers. You Americans play better with shoes on anyway." He smiled.

"I'm not sure you'd want me out there," this was difficult for me to say.

"If I didn't want you there, I wouldn't invite you."

I thought about this for a second. Ricardo didn't have to invite me, but he did. I had to show up. "All right, cool," I said. "I'll be there."

"OK, cool," Ricardo repeated me and smiled. "And how does the saying go in English? You have to play the best to be the best. So it will be fun for you." I nodded. "You just need to get used to the Brazilian style."

"What does that mean?" I asked, stepping onto the sidewalk.

"Come to Palácio de Maria next week and find out." He started to pull away. "Why do Americans say cool?"

"It's like muito bom, it's like a thumbs up." I put my thumb up and laughed.

"OK, I'll see you at the Palácio de Maria, Skidder. Cool?" Ricardo shouted as he drove away.

"Cool." I said.

That same evening, Dad and I were walking along the Copacabana boardwalk. Mom and Keri had been out shopping and we were meeting them for dinner in a few hours. We stopped at one of the beach vendors to have some coconut milk.

Dad and I still hadn't talked a whole lot about our family being in Brazil. I found it easier to avoid the subject. Dad asked me all the time how I was getting along. I just told him that I was fine. The truth was, though, I wasn't fine.

In my frustration after the difficult camping weekend, I decided to figure something out. "You know, I never really asked you what we're doing down here. I mean, I know there was this job offer. Why were you looking at Brazil in the first place?"

Dad was quiet for a minute as he looked off into the ocean. We sat down together on a bench and he began. "We just wanted to live our lives again. Your Mom and I both loved the life we had in San Francisco. But it was becoming a routine. You know?" He smiled. "And now, that routine is the furthest thing from our minds."

"Yeah, you and Mom seem real happy down here."

"We are. I'm glad you've noticed. We also knew that Keri was at an age where moving wouldn't be too big of a deal. The X-factor in this whole thing was you. The only reason we did this is because we know you. You're a special kid. We knew that you could handle this. So tell me Jas, how *are* you handling this?" Dad paused. "If all this rubs you the wrong way, we can be back in San Francisco by next year." I realized how selfless my father was being. He was the happiest I'd ever seen him, but he would trade it all if I asked him to. I couldn't stay angry with him.

Angry or not, though, this was my big chance at an escape. *I could be back playing for Coach Hansen at Hilltop High School next season. I could be playing in another tournament with Bayside United in a year!* These thoughts swirled in and out of my head. But so did other thoughts, like Mariana, Mom, and Dad. I'd only been here for a few weeks. They hadn't been the best weeks of my life, but I couldn't give up yet. And I was interested in the fact that I had so much ground to make up in soccer.

I sat for a moment watching two young boys juggle a soccer ball nearby. Something inside my head clicked. I thought back to how I had watched the soccer games in the park my first day in Rio. Seeing that talent made me realize just how much Brazil could help my game. I remembered Ricardo's words: *you have to play the best to be the best.* These words inspired me. All I needed now was the guts to go for it. Going back to America would be denying myself the opportunity to become a great soccer player. Here in Brazil, the sky was the limit. I'd be competing against the best players in the world. Sure, adjusting to Brazil was going to be challenging. But right there on that bench I decided to accept it.

I turned to Dad and spoke with confidence. "Everything's great, Dad. Or at least it will be."

CHAPTER SEVEN

TRYOUTS

Dad's escape offer made me realize that I hadn't given Rio a chance. The time had come to stop fighting Brazil. It's funny how making a decision to be happy can really change everything. For me, my new attitude affected every area of my life. Most importantly, it fixed my relationship with my Dad. We were buddies again, hanging around one another even more than we had in San Francisco.

And the camping trip made me realize something too. I didn't have time to whine about my soccer game. I needed to do the work and get better. Over the next few months, I played every day at Palácio de Maria. This was my formal introduction to Brazilian futebol. As Ricardo said, this was my chance to learn from the best. Plus, it helped my Portuguese. Through futebol, I slowly began to speak the language more fluently.

When I initially played games at the Palácio, I was the worst player on the field. If too many guys showed up, I wouldn't even be picked for a team. Unless Ricardo was a captain, that is. If I did get picked, my teammates would play around me. It was like this for the first week or so, but slowly I began to improve. I started to understand the way futebol was played in Brazil.

Ricardo and I became buddies. He took me under his wing, always making sure to translate Portuguese into English. I was surprised at how quickly it happened, but in just a few months I considered him a true friend. Not that I forgot about my American friends. I talked to them on e-mail every day. I tried to explain just how good the players were down here. Only when Bones and Kyle visited me for a week did they truly appreciate the skill level of the Brazilians.

They arrived at the airport during the first week of October. We got a chance to play at the Palácio a lot during their visit. Bones held his own in goal, but Kyle was truly humbled. People were stealing the ball away from him and nobody was fooled by his fancy footwork.

After that first game, he begged me to play again the next day. Kyle wouldn't shut up about how lucky I was. "You're so lucky to be able to practice against these guys. You get to play eleven on eleven every day!" After my friends went home I thought about what Kyle had said. And the next time I played at the

Palácio I really did feel lucky.

By December, six months into my life in Brazil, my skills had really improved. I was like a sponge, taking it all in. I watched the players' movements, the way they passed, their feet and their perfect timing. I learned how they were able to put so much swerve on the ball. Slowly, a new understanding of futebol was alive inside of me. My entire game began to transform. I was playing more like a Brazilian. At the Palácio, I was always one of the first five or six guys picked. People knew who I was and they respected me as a player.

"I think I got it, Ricardo." I spoke as we sipped fruit juice outside the gates of the Palácio de Maria. I'd just gotten off the field after playing one of my better games.

"Got what?" Ricardo asked, smiling at a pretty girl passing by.

"I think I understand Brazilian futebol." I spoke with pride in my voice.

"You do, do you?" Ricardo asked, turning to face me with a curious expression.

"It's like this," I dove in, explaining every detail I'd witnessed. The quick, short passes to advance up the field. And the playful nature in which Brazilians toyed with the ball. Then there was the fancy footwork, which was an art form for players like Ricardo. I continued, "I guess the biggest difference is that Brazilians play the game on their toes. The rest of the world is stuck somewhere closer to the heel."

Ricardo smiled. "You're missing something, Skids. It's the secret ingredient."

I had to think about this. I noticed a million differences, but they all boiled down to speed and control of the ball. Ricardo could tell I was lost. "What about my face when I'm playing futebol?"

"You're always smiling, laughing, and joking around."

"There you go."

"What do you mean? You're actually annoying sometimes." I laughed at this comment.

"That's because you haven't grown up with this. I've watched American soccer," at this word, Ricardo cringed. "The players are so serious on the field, like you and your friend Kyle. You might as well be wearing suits and ties out there. I mean, you don't look like you're having any fun. Why is that?"

"Well, for one, it's because we play to win…" Ricardo glanced up at me and raised his eyebrows. I realized instantly that I'd made a mistake. After all, Brazil has won the World Cup five times. They are among the most successful countries every single year. America has never even played in the finals, let alone won the World Cup.

"OK, I'll spell it out for you Skids. For Brazilians, futebol is fun. It's our entertainment. It's a *game* and we treat it like one. Every time I'm playing, I feel a positive energy and I can't help but smile. So I play well, because it is more fun to play well."

I nodded. Ricardo was saying that my basic approach to futebol was non-Brazilian. He was right. I knew that was something I'd have to fix. I gulped down the rest of my fruit juice. Then I stared at the blue summer sky. Summer in December—I wasn't sure I'd ever get used to that.

Along with Ricardo and a couple of other players, I started training off the field. We'd run wind sprints on the beach to build strength in our legs. We'd climb giant hills to build our stamina. After a few months of this, I was in better shape than ever before. My new physical strength was reflected in my game. I could run forever and never grow tired. I was getting more and more used to the speed of Brazilian soccer. I didn't turn the ball over as much or appear as slow on defense. My training and new attitude were paying off.

Still, I was shocked when Ricardo asked me if I would be trying out for the Botofogo Juniors team. "I haven't really given it much thought. Aren't they the best junior team in Brazil?"

"The best junior team in the world," Ricardo shot back.

"No way then," I said. "I don't stand a chance of making that team."

"You're a better player than you think you are. Look how much you've improved already. The game comes so naturally to you. You've been here for less than a year. You're already better than most of these guys. And they've been playing their entire lives."

"Thanks." I shrugged my shoulders. "But Ricardo, I've also been playing my entire life."

"Soccer maybe, but not futebol," he said with a smile.

The days were passing quickly since I'd moved to Brazil. Before I knew it, I'd thrown away the Rio calendar I bought at the airport the day I moved here. That was a year ago! I couldn't believe that I had just celebrated my sixteenth birthday. I couldn't believe that I spoke Portuguese or that my favorite fruit was mango. A lot had changed in my life. I'd had thousands of new experiences in that first year.

Even though I wasn't a surfer, Bones had been right about the beaches. They were incredible. I spent nearly every weekend either at Copacabana or Ipanema. I also went with Mariana on a number of road trips. We visited Iguazú Falls, Brazil's version of Niagara Falls. We traveled to the Pantanal, the best place in Brazil to view animal life. All the while I fed my passion for soccer with daily games at the Palácio. Ricardo continued pushing me to try out for the Juniors. Finally, I decided I would give it a shot. *Why not?*

Things with Mariana were good too. After knowing her for over a year, I felt so comfortable with her. I guess some of this comfort had to do with the fact that my family loved her. They thought she was the greatest thing in the world. Keri would lay out by the pool with her for hours. They would swim and talk like sisters. Mariana showed Mom how to make traditional Brazilian meals like Moquêca, a Brazilian fish soup that we ate all the time. And she would spend hours with Dad, talking about old American movies.

And I was a fixture at Mariana's house as well. Her Mom and I would talk about America for hours. She had always wanted to visit, but had never gotten the chance. I told her about San Francisco, New York City, and anything else she asked about. Mariana's dad, Michel, was a math teacher at the high school. He spent hours helping me with my homework. In return, I helped him perfect his English. Although we all had become very close, I had still not met Mariana's brother Mario.

Mario Fernandez del Vasco was a local hero. He played for a pro futebol team and was rarely home. In a year, I never got the chance to meet him. Many people considered the twenty-year-old to be the best young player in Brazil. In a few months he would be starting for Brazil's national team in the World Cup. Mariana told me that Mario was coming home during August and wanted to see me. I was nervous to meet him.

Two days before tryouts for the Juniors, Mariana joined me at the Palácio. It had been a while since she'd seen me play outside of friendly games on the beach. I was eager to show my improvement. I played one of my best pick-up games ever that day. On one of my three goals, I made Ricardo look silly trying to defend me. I could tell by her expression that Mariana was impressed. She ran over to me after the game. "I definitely think you're ready to meet my brother again," Mariana said. "He'll be in Rio tonight."

"Again? I never met him in the first place," I said.

"Yes you did." Mariana quietly responded. "You played against him in the park the first day you got here. Remember that jerk in the yellow shirt?"

"Yeah, but…" *She couldn't be serious, could she?*

"I should have told you, but I didn't want you to hate him. He's usually not like that, Jason. It was just because he'd never met you. My brother looks after me closely. He hated the idea of me having an American boyfriend who didn't speak Portuguese.." She paused, smiling. "Now you speak perfectly and are one of the best players at the Palácio." Her brown eyes twinkled. "So, will you meet him again?"

Although I was confused, there was only one thing I could say. "Of course I will, Mariana."

That evening, I went with Mariana to her brother's house for dinner. I was scared and excited at the same time. On the one hand, last time I met him he wanted to kill me. On the other hand, I had come a long way and truly cared for Mariana. Plus, this was

Mario Fernandez del Vasco! He was one of the greatest soccer players in Brazil. I had to meet him!

After about fifteen minutes in his house, I knew he was really a nice guy. I understood why he acted the way he had a year ago. I wanted to tell him that our fight was meaningless. Before I could speak, Mario apologized for his behavior. Like any older brother, though, he tested me. "What are your goals?" He asked. "Do you do well in school? What do you do for fun?"

These questions, of course, led to a subject we both loved: futebol. We went on to discuss his career and my tryout with the Juniors the following day. Meanwhile, Mariana sat close to us both, jumping in when she saw an opportunity. She was excited that our second meeting was going so well. The conversation was lively and interesting.

Mario was not much older than I was. Yet, he had a house of his own, paid for by his salary as a futebol player. He talked about all the hard work he'd put in to get where he was. He was the first person I'd ever met who actually played futebol for their job. I admired him and listened to every word he said. He fascinated me. Listening to him, I believed that I could be a professional soccer player. This was a dream I had kept hidden from the world since I was twelve.

An hour later, Mario and I were discussing the Botofogo Juniors and Coach Ribiera. Mario explained that he was known for coaching a fast-paced, offensive game. He only played the fastest of the fast. "These Juniors teams play the fastest-paced futebol in all of Brazil. It's what they're known for. If you can hang with their speed you have a chance."

"I hope I can," I said. "Defending quicker players is the toughest thing for me."

"And there are just a few quick players here in Rio, no?" Mario said. He took a large bite of ice cream. "Listen Skids, I'm going to tell you a great futebol secret." I leaned in closer. He continued, "The key to defending Brazilian players, especially the quick ones, is your eyes. Do not watch their feet. Their dancing feet are like fireworks, exploding around you. The best defenders are not blinded by the light." He looked at me. "Watch the ball. No one will ever get past you."

The next day at tryouts, I remembered Mario's words. I concentrated on the ball. Right away, one of the returning Juniors came at me with his feet flashing wildly. I wasn't blinded by the light. I calmly backpedaled, keeping a watchful eye on the rolling ball. After all the fake moves, he tried to get around me to the outside. I beat him to the spot and stole the ball easily. I was able to repeat this play throughout the afternoon. Overall, I was very pleased with that first tryout.

Coach Ribiera broke the players trying out into two groups, A and B. I wasn't surprised when I was assigned to team B the following day. Ricardo had been placed with the A group, along with most of the returning players. There were fifteen players in the A group and twelve in B. Eighteen would make the final cut.

I played well the next day, but I didn't score or do much to stand out. However, I felt that I was in the top half in terms of speed. I knew this would play to my advantage. A few minutes after practice, we gathered in a circle around Coach Ribiera. As different as Brazilian soccer is from the American version, tryouts were exactly the same. Like in America, the coach always thanks everyone for trying out. Then he gives a speech about not giving up. He even told us about a player he'd cut who went on to make Brazil's national team. I could have sworn that Coach Hansen told us the same story. I had to smile. It was like I was magically transported back to San Francisco.

With these words ringing in my ears, I made my way over to the list. I'd given it my best shot. I'd proven to myself that I could hang with the fastest of the Brazilian players. If I didn't make it, I'd be OK. There would be other opportunities down the road. I consoled myself with these thoughts as I ran my finger down the list. I finally got to the S's.

Sancori
Sepaldo
Skidder

My finger fell from the list. I was stunned. I'd made the team. I'd made *the* team. *Now what?* I wondered.

CHAPTER EIGHT

U.S.A.W.C.

When the World Cup arrives every fourth year, soccer fans throughout the world go crazy. The World Cup is the largest soccer tournament in the world. Every country sends their best players to compete. Eventually, there is only one team left, one flag, one country. Englishmen run in the streets draped in red and white. In Italy people gather in plazas to root on their national team. Thousands gather around single television sets in countries like Senegal and Cameroon. But the parties in all these countries combined don't equal the World Cup craziness in Brazil. Faces are painted, flags are flown, and the entire nation watches. There isn't a single person in the streets! When Brazil scores the whole country erupts. Confetti can be seen falling from apartment balconies everywhere. After a victory, grown men cry with pride.

During my second year in Rio, I was lucky enough to experience the World Cup. And I was extra lucky because Brazil was crowned champion. It was unbelievable! Parades and celebrations through Rio's streets lasted for weeks.

I also followed the United States national team. Normally, they didn't make it out of the first round. This year was different. They had some decent team speed and played a defensive style that allowed them to do well. This was especially cool for me because of the e-mails I'd been getting from Bones. He had actually made the team as a seventeen-year-old. He was the youngest American ever to be on a World Cup roster. Bones never got a chance to play, but that didn't ruin his time. He wrote me e-mails once a week.

Around the same time, I was in my first season with the Juniors. Making the team was great, but I didn't get off to a good start. The fact that I was the only non-Brazilian on the team made my situation harder. I simply wasn't getting along with all of my teammates. Ricardo tried to make me understand that their feelings toward me were not personal. They were all hoping to play for their national team one day. The fact that I was an American citizen bothered some guys. Many of them had friends or brothers who they thought deserved a chance with the Juniors. They wondered why Coach Ribiera would keep some American. I would never have the chance to help Brazil's national team.

Coach Ribiera answered these questions simply, "I picked the best eighteen players who tried out. The American was one of them."

I made the team, but I was probably the worst player. I'm sure Coach would agree with that. Every day in practice, he would hound me for making mistakes. He was very honest, and would say things that hurt. "You're not that good, Skids. There are hundreds in Brazil better than you." Then he would give me hope, "But there's something about you, I can see it. We've got to bring it out." Coach didn't care that I was American. He didn't care that I would never play for the Brazilian national team. For him, the Botofogo Juniors were all that mattered.

I didn't get a single minute of playing time in our first eight games. Even *I* began questioning why Coach had chosen me. It was frustrating. From the sidelines, I tried to remain focused on the game. I watched the way our strikers would break on the counterattack. I noticed the passing patterns of our midfielders.

Ricardo had earned a starting spot as our right striker. He was one of our best players. "Your time will come, Skids," he repeated over and over to me. I believed him at first. But as the games went by, I started to doubt I would ever see action.

My time did come in the ninth game. Our starting right midfielder, Nino Sancori, went down with an ankle injury. A minute earlier our center midfielder,

Felipe Nadio, had to leave the game with a pulled hamstring. Felipe had been replaced by Guy Danilo, our top substitute. When Nino went down, we were running low on middies. Coach Ribiera looked down the bench for someone to replace Nino. His eyes stopped on me. "Skidder, get over here," he scowled. Coach was never happy during games.

I nearly fell over my own feet in excitement. "Yeah Coach?"

"You ready?"

I was about to reply with the line, "I was born ready," but I held back. "Yes sir," I said in a confident voice. I had never been so excited to *play* soccer.

"OK, get in there and run your tail off. The second I see you slowing you're back on the bench."

During the rest of that half I played harder than ever before. The score was still tied at zero, but Ricardo and I made some nice plays together. We'd given our center and left strikers good scoring chances.

We talked about strategy for the second half and I caught Coach Ribiera looking at me. He nodded as though he liked what he had seen. His nod energized me for the second half. I played my heart out for him. Finally, my work paid off in the sixty-fifth minute of the game. From the sideline, I'd noticed the opposing team's goalkeeper was a real showboat. He liked to roll the ball underhand to his teammates after making a save. Sometimes, it even appeared that he rolled the ball without looking. No-look passes might work in basketball, but not in futebol.

Our left striker, Marcelus Torihno, sent a shot right at their goalkeeper. He made the save easily. I slowly walked across the midfield line and then started a light jog toward the goalie. A moment later, I watched their right defender jog toward the sideline. He was awaiting the rolled pass from his keeper. I started in a full sprint up the right sideline that moment. Then I ran diagonal at the goal. Sure enough, the goalie turned to roll the pass without a second thought. He saw me at the last second. I was sprinting in between him and his fullback. He was able to slow his throwing motion, but he couldn't fully hold on. The ball slipped away.

He ran out to grab his mistake, but I had a better jump on the ball. I reached it just before he did. My heart pounded as I felt the leather touch my toe. I could see the back of the net, but had no angle. I had to be patient. In one fluid motion, I touched the ball outside the goalie's reach and looked up. In making the steal, I had come close to the end line, but I didn't have a shot. I stopped the ball and turned back. There were two defenders closing in fast. Beyond them, I saw Marcelus charging hard. Quickly, I chipped the ball over the heads of the two defenders. I watched as Marcelus threw his body to the ground and headed the ball into the empty net. I pumped my fist in the air.

That score remained the same for the rest of the game. My teammates congratulated me after the final whistle. I'd finally done something to prove that I belonged. Slowly, my playing time increased. I continued to run around like a madman every time I got on the field. At first, I felt out of control. The more I played, though, the more I got used to the speed.

As a team, we were playing well. We finished first in our league and were seeded number one in the Brazilian Junior Club Tournament. This event brought together the best junior teams from around Brazil. We squared off in the semifinals against Futebol Clube do Belém. Like us, they had gone through the season undefeated.

Our coaches had watched Belém's last game. It was a crushing seven-one victory in the quarterfinals. They said that Belém's players were faster and in better shape than any team we'd seen this year.

"You give any of these guys a centimeter and they'll blow right by you." Coach Ribiera explained. "I haven't said this to many teams I've coached," he continued, "but they'll beat us in any race. We've got to outsmart them."

Belém, however, proved to be as smart as they were fast. They controlled the ball for most of the game. They chipped quick passes around our team and cut through our defense. It was the first time all season we looked outmatched by an opponent. Still, we hung tough. After ninety minutes neither team had scored.

Three minutes into overtime, Coach sent me

into the game. For the rest of overtime, I ran, dove, and slid like my life depended on it. I stole the ball twice and we were able to push up into Belém territory. Both times, their quickness kept us from getting any real looks at the goal. After ninety minutes of regular time and thirty minutes of overtime, neither team had scored. The winner would have to be determined by penalty kicks.

Coach Ribiera was unsure of who would take the kicks. He gathered us around him on the sideline. This was the first time we'd been involved in a game that had gone this far. Coach needed five volunteers. Immediately Marcelus, Ricardo, and Felipe volunteered. Their "no fear" attitudes were perfect for this situation. After a minute of thinking, Calo Sepaldo said he would take one. This left Coach with one more player to choose. Everyone grew quiet. I looked around our circle. There were more than a few players fidgeting. There was no way I would be asked to take the kick. I hadn't even started in the game. I stared straight at Coach. "Skidder, you Americans like this part of the game, no?" Coach was right. For some Americans, the penalty kick was more exciting than the game itself. Not for me, though.

"Yeah, I guess," was all I said. My jaw nearly dropped when I saw Coach pencil my name onto the list.

As the last shooter, I prayed that we would win before it was my turn to kick. There was no such luck. Nine players, five from their team, and all four from ours, made their shots. The final kick would be mine. Make it and there would be more penalty kicks. Miss it and our season was over. *No pressure Skids*, I thought to myself. My knees wobbled as the referee rolled the ball to me. I kneeled down to position it. In doing so, I glanced up at the large crowd of futebol fanatics. They were screaming, yelling, and singing. I was blinded by the flash of a thousand cameras.

Deep breath, relax, Jason. I rubbed my eyes and backed away from the ball. A shudder ran through my body. Despite the fans staring at me, I'd never felt so alone on a soccer field. I realized why futebol players disliked the idea of a game being decided by penalty kicks. This was a team game, not a one-man show! Penalty kicks in futebol made no sense. It was like baseball teams having a home-run derby instead of extra innings. Suddenly, I hated penalty kicks. The referee's whistle awoke me from my trance. This was not the time to think about the rules of soccer. *Just pound it home*. I took a deep breath and started in on the ball.

I hit the shot well, but knew instantly that it wasn't good enough. With just a short dive to his right, the Belém goalkeeper deflected my shot wide. It was the most important save of his life.

I fell to my knees, overcome by a sadness that I'd never felt before. From the corner of my eye, I watched the Belém players celebrate. I closed my eyes and let my head fall into my hands. Everything became quiet. I couldn't hear the crowd anymore.

I didn't move for an hour. By the time I removed my head from my hands, the fans had all left. Mariana came down and sat beside me. She put her arm around me. I thought about how I'd let my team down. We'd come so far, and worked so hard. Now it all meant nothing. I dwelled on that thought for a while.

In the middle of all my anger and shame, a light broke in. Sure I was upset, but it was only because of how much I cared about the game. It wasn't the losing that upset me the most. It was the fact that our season was over. Tomorrow, I wouldn't be out practicing with my teammates. Once I understood this, I realized how important futebol was to me. I was about to say something, but Mariana spoke first. "You played a good game, Skids."

"I know," I replied.

"I know how seriously you take this game." Mariana seemed to pull those words from inside my brain.

I grabbed her hand and we walked off the field together.

The next night, I read another one of Bones' e-mails about his time with Team U.S.A. It put me in a good mood. He told me about the new soccer balls they used in practice every day. He said that his goalie uniform was custom-made to fit his body. How cool was that? Everything he said made me think about getting back to the States. I wanted my own custom-fitted, starred and striped uniform.

Mom was making dinner when I sat down with her and munched on a mango. "You know, in four years, Mom, I could be playing for Team U.S.A. in the World Cup." I was half joking, of course. But really, there was nothing I wanted more. The problem was that I lived in Brazil.

Mom looked up and without a hint of a smile said, "That's a great goal, Jason. I'm sure you will. I know everyone says this, but you can do anything you put your mind to."

I wanted to tell her that I was kidding. *She must not understand how hard it is to make a World Cup team. She must not realize that I am thousands of miles away from America. She must not understand that no American coaches had ever heard of me.* I started to speak. I wanted to tell her how impossible this was, "Mom, you know…"

She cut me off, knowing what I was thinking. "Just because the odds are against you doesn't mean anything. Write down your dream," she added. "Sometimes goals go unachieved because people forget about them."

I went up to my room and sat down at my desk. I thought about my conversation with Kyle back when I was twelve. We'd talked about this dream back then.

I thought about Mario and the road he had traveled. When he was my age, he was playing on the Juniors too. I thought about Coach Hansen and his words of encouragement. Even Coach Ribiera saw something in me. *So why don't I see it?*

Right then, a surge of confidence ran through my body. For a moment, I did see it. I really could play for Team U.S.A. I pulled a single white index card from my top drawer. *What was I supposed to write down?* I didn't want anyone else reading this. I thought for a second, then wrote a simple little code that would change my life: "U.S.A.W.C."

CHAPTER NINE

HOMECOMING

Two weeks after high school graduation, Mariana and I were talking about the future. We had some pretty big decisions to make. Mariana wanted to begin medical school at the Universidad Federal do Rio de Janeiro. She was also accepted to Southern University in North Carolina, but wasn't sure about attending college in the States. She always said that she'd become a doctor someday. And she was now on her way.

As for me, I'd been accepted to two colleges in Brazil and two in the United States. Luckily, I'd earned full soccer scholarships to all four of them. This was going to be a tough decision. After all, I loved Brazil, and I loved Mariana—but I was an American. I knew that the only chance I had at playing in a World Cup was if I went back to the United States.

On the other hand, I *could* try and make a living playing soccer here in Brazil. I was at a crossroads and decided to let fate decide. If I made the United States World Cup team, I would move back home. If I didn't, I would stay here in Brazil with Mariana.

While sitting in my room, Mariana interrupted my thoughts. "What's U.S.A.W.C. stand for?" She flipped through a pile of index cards, each with a goal I had set. It had been a few years since I'd written down that code. What it stood for hadn't left my mind for an instant.

After about thirty seconds of looking at the card, her eyebrows rose. "So, you really want to play in the World Cup?" she said.

"Well, I'd like to, sure." I could feel myself turning red. I was embarrassed to dream such a big dream before my nineteenth birthday. She put the card away and we sat in silence for a minute. Neither of us spoke about what would happen if she stayed in Brazil and I moved to the States.

I didn't make a big deal about the World Cup to Mariana. The truth was, though, I'd looked at that card every day during the past two years. It was my motivation before so many training sessions and Juniors games.

Just two years removed from my penalty shot miss, we won the championship. Unlike my first season, I was a star player during my second and third. I led the way as we went on to get revenge on Belém in the finals. Meanwhile, Ricardo was developing into one of Brazil's brightest futebol stars. In fact, there were a number of Botofogo players being scouted for the Brazilian national team. Coach Ribiera pulled me aside and told me that a coach had asked about my citizenship.

"He asked what?" I said, hardly able to control myself. This was the Brazilian national team!

"He asked me if either of your parents might be part Brazilian," Coach Ribiera responded. "I told him no, that 'Skidder bleeds the red, white, and blue of America.'" He laughed, pleased with his line.

If the mighty Brazilian national team was interested in me, Team U.S.A. could definitely use me. I thought this was obvious. But living in Brazil over the past four years proved to be a disadvantage. I realized this after sending a highlight tape to Team U.S.A.'s coach, John Gregson. Two weeks after I sent the tape, I received a letter that didn't offer much promise:

Dear Jason Skidder,

Thank you for sending the tape. As you may know, most of the players we take come from our under twenty one national team. Additionally, most of these players are based in the United States. They have been playing together for the past few years in preparation for 2006. This is not to discourage you, but to give you a realistic idea of how difficult making Team

U.S.A. for this upcoming World Cup will be. I'll continue to monitor your progress.

> Best of luck,
> Coach Gregson

It sounded like he was preparing me for the disappointment of not making the team. Still, I believed in myself and continued to read the U.S.A.W.C. goal card every morning. I also knew that I had friends pulling strings for me back in the States. Bones had been named the starting goalie. And Kyle was a star striker on the under twenty one national team. Both of my old friends had spoken with Coach Gregson on my behalf. They told him that I was a player who deserved a closer look.

"He says he'll keep his eye on you. He also mentioned that the national team is deep at midfield." Kyle explained to me over Instant Messenger, our main form of communication.

"Deep! They're as deep as a puddle," I wrote back. "Half those guys are coming back from injuries."

"I'm just passing along his words. At least he said that he's looking forward to seeing you play in person in a couple weeks."

"Well, that's good. At least I have one chance to shine."

"Yeah," Kyle wrote, "big day for you. No time

to choke—just kidding."

The big day Kyle was referring to was May 22. With the World Cup coming soon, there was a lot of soccer to be played. A series of friendly matches were to be held in Dallas between international club teams. The Botofogo Juniors would play an exhibition game against U.S.A.'s under twenty one national team. It would mark the first time I'd played soccer in America in nearly four years.

It would also be a small reunion for Kyle, Bones, and me. Kyle had come down to visit Rio at least once a year since I got there. But I hadn't seen Bones in three years. Seeing old friends was going to be nice. More importantly, though, this was my chance to impress Coach Gregson. I had to be great. In the weeks leading up to the game, proving myself was all I could think about. I was determined.

Standing in the tunnel before the game, I'm not sure if I had ever been more focused. I stared straight ahead and tried to picture what it would be like playing versus Americans again.

"Hey, there's Tom Fool Skidder," I cringed. I turned to see whom the joker was. I was surprised to see an older gentleman standing behind me. It took me a second to figure out who it was. And then…"Coach Hansen! What are you doing in Dallas?"

"Friends and family," Coach said, pointing to the boy who stood at his side. "And to see you and

Kyle play. Talk about never in a million years." He continued, "I always knew you guys were good, but this is beyond my wildest dreams."

"Mine too," I nodded.

He stared off into space for a minute and stroked his beard. "Well, you've got a game to play. I just wanted to see if I could catch you. Give me a call when this is over. I'd like to catch up." He handed me his number on a sheet of paper and took his grandson by the hand. I tucked his number in the inside of my right cleat. Now I had another reason to play well today. Coach Hansen believed in me before anyone did, even before I believed in me.

Warming up, I looked across at the Under Twenty-One national team and saw more then a few familiar faces. There was Kyle and Bones of course. I also recognized Rube Jones, the player who broke Kyle's ankle in the Florida tournament.

As the referee positioned the ball at midfield, we awaited the starting whistle. I motioned to Rube and called out to Kyle. "You play with *that* guy after what happened in Florida?"

"Oh, Rube's alright," Kyle laughed. "Rather play with him than against him."

I looked over at Rube hitting himself in the chest to get fired up for the game. The whistle blew and our opponents kicked the ball into play. It was obvious from the beginning that the Americans were going to play a defensive strategy. Rube was lined up at left fullback and would be marking Ricardo all day. I played behind Ricardo, easing the pressure.

With our superior speed, we controlled the ball and much of the game's tempo. The Americans had nine defenders back, with Bones in goal. This made scoring very tough. Early in the game, we settled for some long-shot attempts. Ricardo and I advanced the ball up the right sideline a few times. In each case, Rube would throw his two-hundred-pound body in the mix, sending us flying. It was turning into a rough game. The crowd's taunting was equally frustrating..

We were faster than the Americans and more skilled too. Still, the score remained tied at zeros. Working the left side of the field, Marcelus made a move past two defenders. He broke up the sideline unguarded. I watched as Ricardo angled into the box to await the cross. I followed about fifteen steps behind. Marcelus sent a low, hard cross into the middle. The ball was headed directly at Ricardo, as were Rube and two other defenders. They realized that our best offensive player was about to get a look at the goal. Bones took a step to his right, readying himself for Ricardo's shot.

While the American team ran at Ricardo, I followed behind him. I'd been playing with him for a long time. I knew he wouldn't shoot. As the three defenders crashed down on him, Ricardo calmly faked a shot and stepped over the ball. This play is called a "dummy" and Ricardo pulled it off perfectly. Every

American defender that had moved over to stop him was now out of position. Even Bones was a step out of place.

The ball rolled to my feet. I controlled it and unleashed a powerful shot that found the upper right corner of the goal. Three years ago I would have been in awe of the shot I'd just made. I smiled immediately and hugged my teammates. I remember looking over at Bones and Kyle, who were watching me celebrate. I never celebrated when I was in America. Like Ricardo said, I was more business like. That was back when I was an American soccer player. I now played Brazilian futebol.

My smile faded as I jogged back to midfield. On the way, however, I glanced over and saw the American coaches pointing at me. I even noticed Coach Gregson making a note. *Keep it up Skids and he'll have to take you*, I told myself.

Despite our one-zero lead, the rough defensive play continued in the second half. Rube kept to his strategy of manhandling Ricardo and me. The crowd was growing antsy. They knew their team needed a goal.

Ten minutes into the second half, the ball rolled out of bounds. I quickly grabbed it for a throw-in. I lobbed the ball into Ricardo and received a one-touch pass back from him. Before I could do anything with the ball, I sensed a shadow charging me. I turned, but was too late. Rube Jones came barreling into my lower body. His cleats were high and I felt a pain shoot up my leg instantly. I fell to the ground hard. Right away, I remembered my last meeting with Rube. That time, it was Kyle who lay injured as a result of a dirty slide tackle.

I can't really tell you what happened next, but something inside of me snapped. I'm not sure if it was bad memories, the crowd's boos, or what. In that moment, I did the only thing I regret doing on a soccer field. Knowing that Rube was still over me on the ground, I threw my elbow into his chin. The blow sent him flying off me. It had been a split-second decision. When I felt my elbow connect with Rube's face, I knew I'd made a mistake.

What followed was a complete blur. The ref came sprinting over with a red card waving high over his head. I'd been ejected from the game. Rube stood up and charged me. He shoved me to the ground as I tried to get up. This set off some pushing and shoving between teams. When calm was restored, I tried to stand. The pain in my ankle was unbearable. I couldn't walk. A stretcher was called and I was carted into the locker room. This wasn't how I'd planned my return to soccer in the United States.

Fifteen minutes later I was icing my ankle from the sidelines. The game changed after that. The American team was able to control play with a one-man advantage. Kyle found our net twice and Bones survived our hard push. The under twenty one Americans held on for a two-one victory.

After the game, my first apology was to my teammates. I had allowed my emotion to get the better of me. I felt as if I'd let everyone down. My teammates were very understanding. The harder apology to make was in the American locker room. I knew I'd made a mistake and was sure that Bones and Kyle would forgive me. The rest of these guys were people I hoped to call teammates. I didn't want them thinking I was a jerk. On a fresh set of crutches, I dragged myself into their locker room. I received a number of glares. Rube's and my eyes met for a second. Fortunately, Kyle and Bones saw me from across the room and came to my rescue.

"What happened out there?" Kyle bumped knuckles with me. I knew he had forgiven me.

"I don't really know. That was horrible," I barely whispered. "I can't believe myself."

A booming voice called out from across the locker room. "Jason Skidder, get in here," Coach Gregson stood tall. He motioned for me to follow him into his office. I limped across the locker room as players continued eying me.

Coach Gregson shut the door behind me. "Have a seat, son. Rube got you pretty hard in the ankle. How's it holding up?"

"Not all that well, sir," I said. I lifted my warm-up pants to reveal my freshly black and blue ankle.

"It was a rough game—two good teams playing hard. That's the kind of intensity I like to see between the lines," he leaned back in his chair. "What I don't like to see is that elbow you threw. There's no place for that."

I nodded but was afraid to speak. I had put myself on thin ice with Coach Gregson when I elbowed Rube. An invitation to play for Team U.S.A. was getting more and more unlikely.

He continued, "When I saw that, I thought, 'here's a guy who has zero control over himself. He goes out and gets thrown off the field and lets his entire team down. Is this the type of character I'd want to coach?' And the answer to that is definitely not. Especially when we're out there representing America."

I was on the verge of tears. My U.S.A.W.C. goal was down the drain.

"I'll tell you what though, Skidder, you've got friends in the right places." Coach Gregson's voice calmed. I looked up at him through a glaze of tears. "Bill Hansen was my commanding officer in the Navy. Luckily for you, he was your high school coach. I respect him more than anyone. He came in here after the game and spoke on your behalf. He told me I hadn't seen the real Jason Skidder out there. Told me you deserved another chance. I didn't agree with him, but I gave in."

A relieved smile passed across my face. "Thank you, Coach. I…" He cut me off. "You're obviously a talented player. I don't think anyone that saw you play out there would dispute that. So I'm inviting you to play in our World Cup tune-up games next April. If you play well there, we'll see. You'll still play out the rest of this year with your club team in Rio. But there is one condition, and I'm dead serious about this. If you pick up another red card this year, the invitation is off. Do you understand me?"

The pain in my ankle was suddenly gone. I smiled through my tears. "Yes, Coach. I promise I won't let you down again."

CHAPTER TEN

THE ZONE

A weird thing happened when we were landing in Rio. I had the feeling that I was coming home. Up until that point, I'd always thought of America as home. Suddenly, the two had flip-flopped. Don't get me wrong, I still thought of myself as an American. The thought of representing the country of my birth in the World Cup was more than an honor—it meant everything to me.

That evening, Mariana and Ricardo came over for a barbecue at my house. After stuffing ourselves, we sat around and talked in my backyard. The mango trees swayed and the tropical birds chirped. We joked and laughed with my parents and Keri. I looked at my two friends and realized just how important each was to me. Mariana was the love of my life, alongside soccer, of course. And Ricardo was the greatest player I had ever seen. (He was even better than Mario, Mariana's brother. Not that I told her that.)   When I first got here I was afraid I'd never find friends. I smiled, sitting on my porch with two of my best friends. I felt as though life could not have been any better.

Ricardo smiled "Have you told them?"

"Told us what?" Mom and Mariana turned to me at the same time.

I smiled, embarrassed. It wasn't that I was purposely hiding the news. I just hadn't found the right moment. I guess this was it. "Well, Coach Gregson invited me to play with Team U.S.A. next year. Just in some exhibition games. But I'm not on the World Cup roster yet. So don't get too…" I was cut off as Mom grabbed me.

"Jason, I am so, so, *so* proud of you," she said into my ear. I looked over her shoulder and caught my father wiping a tear from his eye.

"I'm not there yet, though," I added. "I still need to play well in these exhibition games."

I looked over at Mariana. She had tears in her eyes as well. Her tears were different, though. They were happy and sad tears. If I made the team, I would probably be attending college in America. Our future together was as uncertain as my status with Team U.S.A. I looked into her eyes and we both shared a forced smile.

Dad chimed in. "Jason, you should consider it an honor that you were even invited to try out." My eyes never left Mariana's.

I meant what I said to Mom. I hadn't made anything yet. There was still a huge hurdle to clear. With this in mind, I spent much of the next year training. I trained harder than ever before. My training combined with a healthy diet helped me add fifteen pounds of muscle. At one hundred and eighty pounds, I would no longer be an easy target.

Our Botofogo team didn't do as well as we had in past seasons. Some of our star players, including Ricardo, had become professionals. They'd moved to Brazil's Premier League or to leagues in Europe. I constantly reminded myself to stay hungry and push harder. I also was sure to remain aware that I was one red card away from being left off Team U.S.A.

Fortunately, I finished the season without any incidents. Before I knew what had happened, I was on a flight to Washington, D.C. This was the sight of the first Team U.S.A. exhibition game. My situation was straightforward. We would play three exhibition games over six days. There were twenty five of us competing for eighteen positions. I was right on the bubble.

When I put on my Team U.S.A. uniform I was very excited. Our first test was versus South Korea. They had shocked the world by advancing to the semifinals of the last World Cup. Our coaches decided to play the starters for most of that first game. The game ended in a two-two tie. I was frustrated from the bench. I wanted to play. *Stay focused,* I reminded myself.

The second game against Belgium came and went. Again, I sat the entire game. I watched my teammates sub into the game. I was the only player not to see action. *Maybe Coach Gregson had only included me as a favor to Coach Hansen. Maybe he didn't believe in me.* I began to question whether all my hard work had been worth it.

I felt stupid during phone conversations with my family, Mariana, and Ricardo. I hadn't seen one minute of playing time yet! What could I say to them? My heart sank in these moments. All I could do was wait. I'd come all the way from Brazil and I wasn't even getting a chance!

Over the next day and a half, I debated whether or not to confront Coach Gregson. I wanted desperately to ask him if I would play in our final game. But the last thing I wanted to do was upset him. He was the man who held my soccer destiny in his hands. I decided to hold my tongue and hope.

The final exhibition game was against Mexico's national team. The game was held in San Diego. There were thousands of Mexican fans. They chanted in support of their team. The American fans did their best to compete with the Mexicans. Coach Gregson hadn't said a word to me all afternoon. I figured I would spend another evening on the bench. But three minutes before the game, Coach approached me. "You'll be starting at left midfield tonight, Skids." I nodded. He continued, "I know it's not your natural position. We're loaded on the right side and I want to see how you can handle the left."

"Yes sir," I said, trying hard to conceal my excited grin. The roar of the crowd grew louder. I closed my eyes and tried to concentrate. *This is it Jason. This is the moment you've been waiting for.* My stomach was clenched as I followed my teammates onto the field.

I stood waiting for the referee's whistle to start the game. A chill shot up the back of my neck when play began. It took me a few minutes to get into a rhythm with my American teammates. The style was a bit different from what I had grown used to in Brazil. It was slower with longer passes. We moved around the midfield and Mexico did the same. Neither team was making any good runs. I continued jogging around and passing the ball. *C'mon Skids, get aggressive!* I yelled at myself.

The ball rolled in my direction and I stopped it. From my right, I felt the Mexican midfield close in on me. I spun and looked back to our left defender who was awaiting my pass. This would have been the safe play. Instead, I put my cleats down on top of the ball and rolled it backward. The Mexican player bit on my fake. I turned upfield and had a good amount of space in front of me. The space, however, closed quickly. Mexico's right fullback came to challenge me. Right away, I flipped a short pass to James Fenton, our center midfielder.

The fullback turned back to James. I continued on and blew right past him. Those sprints in the deep sand of Brazil were paying off. I could feel my feet moving faster than ever before. Fenton recognized the give-and-go move. He sent a soft pass up the left sideline. I controlled it easily and was alone on a breakaway. I felt the seventy-five thousand fans stand on their feet and collectively hold their breath. Kyle and our other forward, Cade Thomas, sprinted toward the penalty box. This was our chance to draw first blood.

With my left foot, I belted the ball low and hard into the box. Kyle went airborne and tried to volley it into the goal. The ball was just beyond his reach. It skipped once and from nowhere, Cade slid in and pounded it past the goalkeeper.

One to zero, Team U.S.A.

The American fans went crazy. The Mexican fans sat stunned. As soon as he'd stood up, Cade ran over to me. He was followed by the entire team. "Hey, where have you been?" He asked with a smile. "Great pass!"

I laughed but didn't speak a word. The fact that I had contributed felt great. I knew I needed to play solid for the entire game if I wanted to impress Coach Gregson. I settled back into the game and waited for my next opportunity. I knew one would come, but I was shocked when it came so soon.

Less than two minutes after Cade's goal, Mexico got sloppy and turned it over. Fenton toyed with the ball as Kyle tried to make a short run. Fenton sent a pass in to Kyle, but a defender got a foot on it and the ball ricocheted into the open field. I'd been floating behind the action. The ball rolled toward me and toward a Mexican defender behind me. I sprinted and felt him on my heels. When I reached the ball, I would have to make a quick decision. If I dribbled, he would have an easy chance at a steal. I knew that I had a split second to make a play. With no passing lanes open, shooting seemed to be my only option. I was probably close to sixty feet from the goal. I ran in at full speed and hammered the ball with everything my right foot had. It was by far the hardest I had ever kicked a soccer ball.

At worst, I figured, the ball would go out of bounds or the goalie would make the save. At best, maybe there could be a rebound and a chance for Kyle or Cade. Never did I think I could score from out there.

The goalie must not have either. From his reaction it was clear I'd surprised him. The ball shot through the penalty box like a white laser. It screamed by the heads of two Mexican defenders who leapt up. By the time the keeper made a dive, it was too late. The ball found the upper-left corner of the goal and the net rippled like the ocean.

Two-nothing, Team U.S.A. I had a goal and an assist already—not a bad day at the office. Heck, this was my best day at the office ever! I wanted to jump out of my skin I was so excited.

I've heard athletes talk about finding the "zone" during competition. They say that everything slows down and the difficult becomes easy. I'm not sure if I was in the zone that night, but I didn't feel normal. Players around me looked like they were moving in slow motion. I could move around a defender and steal the ball easily. My passes were perfect. I was the fastest guy on the field. With Coach Gregson looking, I went on to score again. And just before the final whistle blew, I assisted on our final goal. I was involved in all four goals and had played the game of my life.

Everyone congratulated me after the game, even Rube. Everyone, that is, except Coach Gregson. He stormed off the field into his office as he did after every game. I decided not to think about it. I had gone out and done the best I could. Now all I could do was wait and hope it was enough.

My high didn't leave as I showered and changed after the game. Television cameras and reporters circled my locker. They wanted to know everything about my life. *Who was I? Where had I come from? How had U.S. soccer missed me?* The questions were fast and the lights were bright. I was enjoying every second of this attention. Every answer I gave to the reporters was filled with stories about Brazil. I talked about the Rio skyline, soccer on the beach, mangoes, and becoming a futebol player at the Palácio. It was "Brazil this" and "Brazil that." I started to understand how important my experience down there had been.

When the lights and the reporters vanished, Coach Gregson's loud voice shot across the locker room. "Skidder, can I see you for a minute?"

"Sure coach," I walked into his office. This time, my head was held high. I took a deep breath before opening the door. *No matter what happens in here, you'll be fine,* I said to calm myself.

I took a seat in the office chair facing his desk. Coach leaned back and stared at the ceiling. He wiped sweat from his head. He struggled for words. I was sure that despite my performance, he was going to cut me. He looked at me for a few moments. It wasn't the kind of look that gave anything away. Coach opened and closed his desk drawer. And then he just looked at me silently. It was the kind of silence that could break you. I'd heard it before; it was the silence of waiting. I'd spent sleepless nights in this silence. I'd waited for Brazil, waited to make a team, waited for a phone call. Each time I stood poised for a straight kick, life would put some swerve on it. This time, I was ready either way.

"Uhhhh," he finally sighed. "Skids, you're the type of kid who makes my job so difficult." *What was he getting at*? "I owe you an apology. I never had any intention of putting you on my team after that red card. Now if I don't include you, I think the team would run me out of town. Heck, after the way you played today, I'd run myself out of town." My legs went numb as he said the next words. "Welcome to Team U.S.A., son, you earned it."

A single tear rolled down my cheek. I took a deep breath to keep the floodgates from opening. But I couldn't keep them closed for long. I thanked Coach for the opportunity and made it out of the room. Two steps later I crumpled to the floor. I was overcome with emotion. I'd done it! U.S.A.W.C. was no longer a dream. The World Cup would begin in a few short weeks. And I was playing!

CHAPTER ELEVEN

GAME DAY

Game day, baby, game day! It was the first thought I had as I opened my eyes. We were playing our first game that afternoon in beautiful Munich, Germany. It would be a tough game, especially for me personally. Our opponent was the most feared team on the planet. It was also the country I once called home—Brazil.

Sitting on the field before the game, I stretched my leg muscles. I thought about how good it felt to be here. I was wearing the red, white, and blue and couldn't think of three better colors. More importantly, this uniform was fitted just for me. There was nothing more comfortable, no piece of clothing I would rather wear. I glanced across the field at Ricardo and gave a smile. I remembered a slow-footed American running for his life on the beach in Boisucanga. Who was that stranger?

Throughout my life, soccer had been there for me. It had given me my highest highs and lowest lows. Despite the roller coaster ride, I'd never lost my passion for the game. I hadn't taken the straightest road to my dream. My life had been a swerve ball.

Scanning the family section of the stands, I found Mom, Dad, Keri, and Mariana. My parents and Keri were decked out in red, white, and blue from head to toe. Mariana sat next to them in the green and yellow colors of Brazil. The good news was that she was wearing an Eastern University hat. She was beginning their medical program next month. Meanwhile, I had signed a contract to play with a professional soccer team in Washington, D.C. and would be going to college at night. I was just a three-hour drive from Mariana. Everything had worked out perfectly for both of us.

I laughed at her in the stands. Even having a boyfriend on the opposite team didn't shake her love for Brazil.

I looked around at all the players and fans. There was no place I would rather chase the king. Kyle and Bones were by my side and the great Ricardo smiled from across the field. He was draped in the yellow and green of my second home. I looked to the top of the stadium. An American and a Brazilian flag whipped across one another in the strong wind. Seeing those two flags flying side–by-side was the most beautiful sight in the world. Talk about a swerve ball!

TEST YOURSELF...ARE YOU A PROFESSIONAL READER?

Chapter 1: Swerve Ball

1. What were some of Skids's immediate feelings when he heard the news that his family was moving to Brazil?

2. Who is Pelé and what does Skids know about him?

3. What is a swerve ball? Why is this chapter entitled, "Swerve Ball?"

ESSAY

In this chapter, life puts some swerve on Skids's plans. How do you think you would react to the news that you and your family were picking up and moving to another country? Do you think Skids handled the situation well?

Chapter 2: Chasing the King

1. Name a pair of observations that Skids made during his first varsity soccer game.

2. What were some of the reasons Kyle mentioned when discussing why he loved the game of soccer?

3. What deal did Skids make with his parents that affected his attitude about the pending move to Brazil?

ESSAY

In this chapter, Kyle introduces Skids to his "chasing the king" metaphor. Explain this metaphor and specifically how "chasing the king" in chess relates to the game of soccer.

Chapter 3: Go For It

1. How did the move to Brazil continuously haunt Skids?

2. Why were Skids and his Hilltop High teammates more rattled than usual when they allowed the first goal against West Mission High School?

3. Do you believe that Skids's "tomfoolery" speech affected the outcome of the game against West Mission? Defend your position.

ESSAY

In this chapter, we read about a friendly rivalry between West Mission and Hilltop High School. What is a rivalry? Detail a rivalry that you might have with another school, an opponent, or a friend.

Chapter 4: A New Friend

1. What was set to happen in Skids's life on June 26?

2. Why was Skids intent on scoring a goal in the game against Texas? Did his personal aspirations help or hurt the team? Explain.

3. How did Mariana assist the Bayside team in their victory over Texas?

ESSAY

Initially, Skids's reaction to the news that he would be moving was not to talk to his parents about Brazil. By the end of Chapter 4, we can see that his perception of the move has changed. His last thought of the chapter is "Bring on Brazil, I can handle anything right now." Name something or someone in your life that you may not have agreed with initially, but that over time, you realized that you misjudged the situation. Detail how your initial reaction changed over that time. What did this teach you?

Chapter 5: Rio

1. What differences did Skids first notice between American and Brazilian soccer players?

2. Cite the differences in seasons between the United States and Brazil.

3. In the Skidder family, who seemed to be the most affected by the move to Brazil?

ESSAY

Throughout the story, we sense that Skids still holds some ill will toward his father for moving the family to Brazil. In this chapter, Skids begins to release these feelings as he accepts the situation. Do you think Skids is justified in being upset with his dad? What would you have done differently, if anything?

Chapter 6: Escape

1. Why was Skids excited to go camping with Mariana and her friends?

2. Why was Skids so embarrassed when he learned that everyone in the car spoke English?

3. Why is this chapter entitled "Escape?"

ESSAY

What did Skids do with his big chance to leave Brazil when his dad offered him the opportunity? What specifically was Skids thinking of when he made his decision? If you were in his shoes, what do you think you would have done with the opportunity to leave? Explain your reasoning.

Chapter 7: Tryouts

1. Ricardo goes out of his way to make Skids feel welcome in Rio.

Cite one example from Chapter 7 to show how Ricardo involves Skids in the Brazilian culture.

2. After Kyle and Bones left Brazil, why did Skids suddenly feel lucky to live where he did?

3. Why do Ricardo and the Brazilians smile when they play futebol?

ESSAY

In this chapter, we read about Ricardo and Mario stepping forward as futebol mentors to Skids. What is a mentor? Name someone in your life that you consider to be a mentor and detail how this person helped you overcome a challenge that you've faced.

Chapter 8: U.S.A.W.C.

1. Why were some of Skids's teammates bothered by the fact that he made the Botofogo Juniors team?

2. What did Skids notice from the sideline—in regards to the other team's goalie—that helped his team score a goal when he finally entered the game?

3. What do the letters U.S.A.W.C. stand for? Why did Skids decide to write them down?

ESSAY

In this chapter, Skids's mom discusses the importance of writing down goals in order to not lose focus. Skids's dream goal was to play in the World Cup. Hard work, dedication, and confidence are essential on the road to accomplishing a dream. Right now, grab a pen or pencil, and write down your dream goal. What character traits will be needed on your road to reaching your dream goal?

Chapter 9: Homecoming

1. Name a few reasons Skids felt that he had to play a solid game on May 22.

2. What was the only thing Skids did on the soccer field that he ever regretted? What do you think made Skids do it?

3. What is a red card in soccer? Why was Skids given the card in the game against the Under Twenty-One American team?

ESSAY

Throughout the story, we have read of the advantages of playing futebol in Brazil. Cite some of these advantages. In this chapter, we learn that there are also some disadvantages to Skids's playing soccer internationally. Cite these disadvantages. Are Skids's chances of playing for Team U.S.A. affected by the fact that he has lived in Brazil and has played soccer there for four years? Explain.

Chapter 10: The Zone and Chapter 11: Game Day

1. What revelation hit Skids as his flight back from the United States approached Brazil?

2. Who held Skids's soccer destiny in his hands?

3. What colors did Mariana wear when Skids and Team U.S.A. competed against Brazil? Why did she wear these colors?

ESSAY

Congratulations! You have completed another Scobre story. In light of this journey, tell us what you learned from the life of Jason Skidder and how you plan on making your own dreams come true. Additionally, if you had to move to a new and unfamiliar place, what lessons from Skids's life could you take along with you?